Brides of Montclair 15

A MONTCLAIR HOMECOMING

The CONCLUDING VOLUME *of the*
BRIDES OF MONTCLAIR SERIES

By *best-selling author*

JANE PEART

ZondervanPublishingHouse
Grand Rapids, Michigan

A Division of HarperCollinsPublishers

A Montclair Homecoming
Copyright © 2000 by Jane Peart

Requests for information should be addressed to:

📖 ZondervanPublishingHouse
Grand Rapids, Michigan 49530

Library of Congress Cataloging-in-Publication Data

Peart, Jane.
    A Montclair homecoming / Jane Peart.
        p. cm. — (Brides of Montclair ; 15)
    ISBN 0-310-67161-2
    1. Women artists—Fiction. 2. Hospitals—Fiction. I. Title.
PS3566.E238 M6 2000
813'.54—dc21
                                         99-088527
                                              CIP

Printed in the United States of America

---

00 01 02 03 04 05 /❖ DC/ 10 9 8 7 6 5 4 3 2

A Note from the Author

WITH THIS BOOK my Brides of Montclair series comes to a close. Unless I were to write a novel about each character, it would be impossible to satisfy all of the specific questions readers have asked over the past fifteen years. Still, I hope at least some of them are answered.

My original intention in writing about the Montrose and Cameron families was to show the personal impact of the historical events of our country on families, relationships, individual lives. I tried to make these stories interesting and to create memorable characters. I never imagined that these books would touch hearts in such meaningful ways, as so many of you have written to tell me they have. These letters have been enormously encouraging and inspiring. I am deeply grateful.

I think we all hope to find the purpose for our life. I thank God every day for giving me work I love and using it in whatever way he chooses.

Thank you for your loyal readership.

Sincerely,

Jane Peart

Part 1

chapter
1

DR. EVAN WALLACE ripped off his latex gloves and tossed them into the waste receptacle. He stepped back from the operating table while the anesthetized patient was lifted onto the gurney, its side rails were adjusted, and the patient was wheeled away to recovery.

He pulled down his surgical mask and raised his strong-featured, deeply tanned face up to the balcony of the fourth-floor operating room, where a group of surgical residents, medical students, and nurses had been observing the surgery. His keen blue eyes scanned the expressions of those leaning forward against the railing.

"Any questions?" he asked. He waited a full minute. When none were raised, Dr. Wallace spun on his heel and left.

After he disappeared through the swinging door, a murmur circulated through the assembled audience—awed comments, complimentary remarks. Watching Dr. Wallace was always an extraordinary experience. The fact that nobody seemed to have a question was due mainly to the fact that while his hands moved he explained each detail of the intricate procedure. When it was completed, there remained nothing but admiration and respect for the surgeon's skill.

9

In the corridor outside, the doctor walked toward the waiting room to speak to the relatives of the patient on whom he had just operated. As he passed the nurses' station with only a brief nod, Ginny Stratton exchanged a significant glance with another O.R. nurse.

Dr. Wallace was an enigma on the floor. He was considered cold, aloof, self-absorbed, detached. He was courteous enough, but he never indulged in small talk or kidding with the nurses at the desk when he stopped to pick up a patient's chart or write orders. No one disputed that he was a dedicated doctor, but in the nurses' opinion he lacked warmth and a sense of humor.

He did not seem to have any close friends among the other doctors on staff, nor did he attend any of the hospital-sponsored social events. If he had a private life—and there was much speculation about this—no one had a clue. All they knew was that Dr. Wallace was thirty-six, single, and drove a red Porsche.

Twenty minutes after Dr. Wallace walked out of the operating room, a yellow cab swerved into the hospital driveway. With a squeal of brakes it came to a jolting stop at the front entrance. Its rear door opened and a slender young brunette emerged, struggling with a large, black artist's portfolio.

Joy Montrose's budget rarely included a taxi. Her usual mode of transportation was her clunky, small economy car or her three-speed bike. However, this morning was special. Today, September 8, 1980, was important. She couldn't risk being late for this interview that might change her whole life.

The driver flipped the meter lever and turned to collect his fare. Joy counted out the bills carefully. So what, she thought, if it meant lunch would be a carton of yogurt for the next few weeks? If she got this job, it would be worth it.

After the cab roared off, she stood for a minute looking up at the U-shaped structure, its two wings projecting like giant arms. Good Samaritan Hospital stood on a hilltop overlooking the Ohio Valley and the city of Middleton. On its staff were some of the nation's best-known health professionals. It had become a symbol of hope to all the sick and suffering who thronged through its doors for help and healing. Patients from all over the United States as well as from other countries came seeking the most modern treatment, care, and possibly a cure. It had a reputation as being a place where miracles sometimes took place.

Joy's gaze moved over to the pentagon-shaped addition, where the morning sun glistened dazzlingly on the windows—the new visitors' solarium in the surgery wing. Her heart hammered. Today she was presenting her paintings to the committee that would make the final selection of the artist to paint a mural for its walls.

A citywide contest had been held and, much to Joy's astonishment, she had made the final cut. Although she knew she was presenting samples of her very best work, she also knew that the competition among the finalists would be keen. It was the chance of a lifetime—albeit a somewhat slim chance. Joy drew a long breath, shifted her portfolio more firmly under one arm, and went up the hospital steps.

Approaching the wall of plate glass leading into the lobby, she saw herself reflected. Today she had carefully "dressed for success." She wanted to give the impression of a serious professional, not a hippie artist. She hoped her simple blazer, skirt, and high-heeled boots projected that image. Her shiny brown hair, usually worn in a braid or ponytail, was swept into a French twist. Despite her efforts, she knew it was hard to look sophisticated at the age of twenty-three. She reminded herself again that the main thing was not her appearance but what was contained in her portfolio.

Joy pushed through one of the doors and walked into the huge lobby. The walls were painted in pastel shades, and vinyl armchairs were placed in conversational groupings around tables upon which current magazines were fanned out. Brass planters filled with lush, green philodendrons provided a backdrop.

Although her experience of hospitals was limited, it was not what she had expected. She had assumed that in a hospital with a reputation like Good Samaritan's there would be more frantic activity, such as she'd seen on TV dramas.

There was no sense of panic or urgency among those milling about. As Joy glanced around, she noted that the overall atmosphere was one of cheerful calm. There was no sense of unusual hurry. People wearing white-and-green jackets moved with brisk efficiency across the polished linoleum floor, going about their professional duties.

Across the lobby a bank of elevators was in constant use, with overhead lights flashing, doors soundlessly sliding open and shut, an ongoing parade of people flowing in and out. There were neon-lit arrows and signs: "Admittance," "Cafeteria," "Gift Shop," "X-Ray," "Radiology."

Joy stood uncertainly for a moment. Then, seeing a circular desk over which hung a sign that read, "Information," she headed in that direction.

The clerk behind the counter told her that the mural selection committee was meeting in the conference room on the fourth floor. Joy glanced at a wall clock. It was nearly a quarter to ten. Very soon all her painstaking preparation and hopeful prayers were going to be put on the line, her work laid out for inspection, critique, comment, and possibly rejection.

Joy prayed for composure. Whatever happened was okay, she told herself. But the truth was, this particular project had spurred her creative energy in a way nothing before had. She honestly believed that her theme for the mural, "The Healing

Miracles of Jesus," was inspired. It had come to her so clearly. What better idea to convey to anxious hearts in the hospital's waiting room than God's message of faith, hope, and healing?

Joy adjusted the strap of her shoulder bag, juggled the portfolio again, and walked over to the elevators.

She pressed the up button, then stepped back into the group of those waiting. A moment later the elevator door opened. Gripping her portfolio, Joy started forward and collided headlong into someone.

The portfolio was knocked from under her arm. She made a futile grab for it, but it went sliding across the polished floor. At that moment she heard a man's voice say, "Sorry. That yours?"

"Yes," she said, hurrying to get it at the same time he did. As she bent to pick it up, they cracked heads. Both straightened up and stepped back, regarding each other warily.

"Are you all right?" he asked.

Momentarily dazed, Joy saw the man she had bumped into with such force. Of medium build, wearing a tweed jacket, he had closely cropped sandy-gray hair and was staring at her with startlingly blue eyes in a tanned face. *A marvelous face to paint*, was her irrelevant thought. Except at the moment he was frowning—scowling, actually.

"No . . . I mean . . . yes. I'm okay." She rubbed her forehead doubtfully.

He picked up her portfolio. "No damage, I hope?"

"I don't think so. It's pretty sturdy."

"Well, here you are," he said and handed it to her.

"I'm sorry; it was my fault."

"No problem," he said curtly.

"I wasn't looking. I was—," she murmured. But she didn't get to finish, because he was already striding across the lobby. Somewhat taken aback by the incident, she watched the trim figure go out through the glass entrance door, then saw him

13

walk toward the section of the parking lot marked "Reserved for Physicians."

At the sound of the elevator doors opening again behind her, Joy quickly pulled herself together and tried to focus on the interview ahead. She stepped inside, and at its upward swoop her stomach lurched. Was it from nervousness, or from dizziness caused by the sharp whack on the head she had just received?

In the parking lot Dr. Wallace turned the key in the ignition, starting the powerful engine of his car. He felt unusually lightheaded. That was a nasty crack on the head he'd taken in the lobby. He rubbed his forehead ruefully. He'd probably given one, too, for that matter. That girl had been as startled as he had at their impact. Her eyes had been wide and dark— she had looked like a deer caught in headlights. Pretty, small, slender. He hoped he hadn't hurt her.

He squinted in the sunlight, reached for his dark glasses, still feeling a little dizzy. Perhaps he should get something to eat, he thought. After all, he'd been up since five that morning and had been operating since seven. What he needed was some breakfast. Coffee, at least. With the meeting at ten o'clock, there wasn't time for much more. Why Dr. Fonteyne, the chief of staff, had asked him to be on the selection committee to choose the artist for the new solarium mural, he didn't know. *What do I know about art or artists?* he thought. In his opinion, medicine and art couldn't be farther apart. Irritated, he shifted into reverse and backed out of his parking space.

In admissions the office manager, Clare Morgan, looked up from her desk as Sister Mary Hope, a member of the hospital ministry from the chaplain's office, poked her head in the door. The nun was a diminutive woman with shiny hair cut in bangs across her forehead, sparkling blue eyes, and cheeks as rosy as a child's.

"Good morning, Sister," Clare greeted her.

"Ready?"

Clare tapped her mouth with her pen. "Ready for what?"

"The selection committee meeting for the solarium mural. We've got three artist applicants coming in today. Did you forget?"

"I did," Clare said, nodding. "This place has been a madhouse this morning. I'll be with you in a minute; just wait while I put these folders in the files."

Clare was in her fifties, with silver gray hair fashionably styled, brushed back from a face that was attractive and probably had once been beautiful. She had a mouth that smiled easily, a laugh that was infectious. Widowed at forty, she had found herself wealthy and with time on her hands which she did not want to fill with empty luncheons, at the country club, or on the golf course. She had first come to Good Samaritan as a volunteer, filling in wherever she was needed. Since she had helped her late husband, a contractor, in his business, knew accounting, and was familiar with every kind of office machine, she was soon offered a job in admissions when the man who had been holding the position transferred to administration. Since then Clare had improved the efficiency of this important part of the hospital.

In pediatrics Dr. Jean Braden's beeper went off just as she was coming off rounds. She stopped at the nurses' station to take the call. It was her office reminding her of the ten o'clock meeting on the fourth floor. Actually, she was looking forward to it. She was the one who had encouraged Joy Montrose to try for the commission. Joy had decorated the office Jean shared with her husband, Dr. Roy Braden. Their young patients, as well as the children's parents, had delighted in the nursery-rhyme and fairy-tale characters Joy had painted. The colorful figures seemed to dance happily all around the walls of the waiting room. Jean would like to see Joy get the job. She stuffed the loop of her stethoscope in one pocket of her lab coat and hurried to the elevator.

Glendon McFarland, the architect whose firm had designed the solarium, pulled into the visitors' parking lot. He glanced at his watch. He'd had to cut short another meeting to make it to Good Samaritan in time, but he hadn't minded. In fact, he'd been pleased that Dr. Fonteyne had asked him to be part of the selection committee. This morning they would be interviewing prospective artists to decorate the pentagon-shaped solarium. It was crucial which artist would be chosen to paint the murals in the wide panels between the plate glass windows. The wrong one could be a disaster, possibly ruining the beautiful simplicity of his design.

At thirty, Glendon was ambitious and anxious. He had just gone into business for himself after working for a big architectural firm for six years. It had been a big leap, but his duties at the large company had been limited mainly to draftsmanship. The firm, which bid on all the city's major jobs, hired people right out of architectural school and put them to work immediately. Glendon had suspected that they did this to cut down on competition. New graduates were full of original ideas, innovative plans, yet few had the connections or the money to strike out on their own. After a few years Glendon had become restless, bored, and frustrated at not being able to use his own creativeness. It had been a real coup to have his design win the commission for the city's prestigious Good Samaritan Hospital.

He checked his wristwatch. It was time to get up to the meeting. He'd meant to be early enough to do a little lobbying, politicking, among the other members. It would be nice to hear a few compliments as well. He meant to have his voice heard in this selection.

Sylvia Thornton, Dr. Fonteyne's secretary, tapped lightly on his office door before entering. "It's almost ten, Doctor."

Jim Fonteyne shoved his horn-rimmed glasses down his nose and looked at her over them, his expression blank. "Ten?" he repeated.

"The artists for the mural interviews," she reminded him gently.

"Oh yes, that." He closed the folder he was perusing at his desk and stood up, a rangy man with iron gray hair, looking younger than his sixty years. He reached for his coat jacket and shrugged his broad shoulders into it. His wife, Lillian, had especially chosen the blue-striped, white-collared shirt and dark blue jacket for him to wear this morning. She always kept track of his appointments, carefully chose the appropriate outfit for whatever he was doing that day, and laid it out for him each morning while he showered.

Sylvia surveyed him critically. She had worked for him for six years and took immense pride in her job with the chief of staff. She understood the prestige of his position. Burdened with the many duties of his work, Jim Fonteyne was careless about himself. That was why his secretary and wife made sure he always looked well put together, well groomed. Dr. Fonteyne knew this and was amused by their contrivance. Now, with a hint of a smile, he asked, "Everything okay, Syl?"

Sylvia nodded and looked on approvingly as he straightened his red paisley tie. Yes, Mrs. Fonteyne would be satisfied.

He walked to the door, then halted and turned back to Sylvia. "Where are we meeting?"

"Conference room, fourth," she replied.

"Yes, of course. Thanks," he said and went out the door.

chapter
2

"Miss Montrose?"

At the sound of her name Joy involuntarily started. She had been sitting in the hall for what had seemed an endless length of time as the other two artists were interviewed. She turned to see an attractive, gray-haired lady standing in the open door of the conference room. "I'm Clare Morgan, from admissions. Won't you please come in?"

Joy stood up, clutching her portfolio, and followed her into a large room, where five people were seated at one end of a long table.

Mrs. Morgan made the introductions. "This is Miss Joy Montrose. And this is the mural selection committee: Dr. Jim Fonteyne, our chief of staff; Mr. Glendon McFarland, the architect who designed the new solarium; Sister Mary Hope, of the chaplain's office; Dr. Jean Braden, whom I believe you know; and Dr. Evan Wallace, chief of surgery."

All the names and faces blurred except one. The man introduced as Dr. Evan Wallace was the man she had collided with coming out of the elevator in the lobby. But if he had a similar recall, he did not show it by even a flicker in his steel blue eyes.

"Now, Miss Montrose, if you'll just take your place over there." Mrs. Morgan indicated a wooden lectern with an easel placed alongside. "The lighting is adjusted so the committee can see your work to its best advantage."

A wave of panic swept over Joy. Her hands, holding the portfolio, were clammy; her fingers felt numb. Here came the real test. This was it, the defining moment of all the weeks of work. They would either like or hate her paintings.

"Thank you for coming, Miss Montrose," the distinguished-looking man introduced as Dr. Fonteyne said. "Would you tell us a little about yourself—your background, your art education?"

Joy swallowed. She was an artist, not a speaker. Probably her experience might seem very thin to this group, depending on the other artists who were submitting their work for this commission. Would anyone care that from the time she could hold a crayon, all she had wanted was to be an artist? That she had drawn, colored, and painted all through elementary school, high school, and junior college? That she had won a year's scholarship to the city's art institute? Or that currently she worked at Shelton's Department Store, setting up displays, decorating windows, printing signs, while continuing to take evening classes?

Another panel member, a youthful-looking woman with an eager, interested expression, spoke. "We understand you have done other murals?"

"Yes, Dr. Braden's office."

Joy glanced gratefully at Jean, who turned to the others, saying, "I would be happy for the rest of the committee to come and see our waiting room after office hours. Miss Montrose created a carousel on which delightful nursery-rhyme characters ride around the room. We've had great response from both our patients and their parents."

"Any other work you'd like to mention? Specifically, murals that could be seen locally?" This came from Glendon McFarland.

"I've worked with a team of students from the art institute on a mural at the Children's Day Center. That's where Dr. Braden saw my work and asked me to design a mural for her office."

"Well, Miss Montrose, perhaps we should see the sketches you've brought for us to examine today, and you could explain your theme," suggested Dr. Wallace.

Did she detect a slight impatience in his tone? Well, she would not let it unnerve her. Saying a silent little prayer, Joy positioned the first of her pictures on the easel. "Since the solarium is pentagon-shaped, with windows between the wall panels, I have chosen to depict five of Christ's healing miracles. The figure of Jesus would only be seen as a shadow or as light. The people being healed would tell their own stories."

One after the other she placed her paintings—all rendered in watercolor on eighteen-by-fourteen-inch illustration board—in sequence as she gave their individual titles: "'Jarius's Little Daughter,' 'The Centurion's Servant,' 'Peter's Mother-in-Law,' 'The Blind Man,' 'The Paralytic at the Pool.'"

"Perhaps you could pass them among the members of the committee so that each could have a closer look?" Mrs. Morgan suggested.

"Certainly," Joy said and gathered them up and handed them to her. As the paintings were passed from one to the other, Joy tried to read some reaction in the individual faces. But it was impossible.

Finally Mrs. Morgan asked, "Does anyone have any further questions for Miss Montrose, or any additional comment he or she would like to make?"

Joy's stomach tightened as she waited for what seemed a long moment. Then Dr. Wallace spoke. "Miss Montrose, I find your sketches interesting, colorful, and professional. No doubt you have talent and the skill to execute your ideas. My question is, would you be willing, if you were the chosen artist for the mural, to change your theme? In other words, to work out another one? The reason I bring this up is because at this hospital we treat all kinds of people, not only Christians, and I wonder if so explicit a religious theme is suitable or appropriate in a nonsectarian institution."

A murmur rippled down the table, members looking at each other. Evidently, that question had not occurred to anyone else. It caught Joy completely off guard. She had never expected such an objection. Again with a silent prayer for help, she met Dr. Wallace's challenging gaze and answered. "Frankly, that possibility hadn't entered my mind. My theme seemed so . . . so right somehow." She paused. "But to answer your question, I think any artist would find it difficult to develop someone else's concept." Was she giving up her chance to paint the mural? For a moment she faltered, seeing her great opportunity slip away from her. Then she lifted her chin and added firmly, "However, since the name of this hospital is Good Samaritan, I believe my theme is perfectly in keeping with the spirit of an institution which treats everyone regardless of race, religion, or creed."

Her gaze swept over the faces of the five people looking at her. All were unreadable except for that of Sister Mary Hope. There seemed to be an affirming twinkle in her eyes, and a smile tugged at her mouth. Joy even thought she saw a flicker of admiration in the eyes of Dr. Wallace.

Amazed at her own boldness, Joy felt a delayed reaction. Her knees suddenly felt as if they were turning to gelatin, and she reached out to steady herself on the lectern.

"Thank you very much, Miss Montrose," Mrs. Morgan said in a tone that declared the interview at an end. "If you will, kindly leave your portfolio so the committee can examine and discuss your work more thoroughly. You will of course be notified either way when the committee reaches its decision."

"Of course."

Joy wasn't sure just how she managed to get out of the room, to the elevator, and back down to the lobby. The next thing she knew, she was standing outside in the bright autumn sunshine.

Without her portfolio, there was no need for the extravagance of a taxi, so Joy started walking to the nearest bus stop.

She had left nearly six weeks of planning, dreaming, praying, and hard work with a group of five people. Win or lose. She had done all she could. Now her future was in the hands of those five people. At least her ordeal was over. The rest was up to the Lord.

chapter
3

THE NEXT WEEK crawled by. The only way Joy was able to survive the suspense was to plunge herself into her work at the store. Luckily, it kept her very busy. There were several new window displays to set up. This required her going to each department to collect merchandise she needed to feature coordinating shoes, handbags, jewelry, scarves, and accessories. She also had to acquire props for the backgrounds. Since she was only one of three assistants to the display manager, Joy rarely was able to create a whole window completely. She followed the written directions and every once in a while had a chance to add a touch of her own. However, the work was demanding enough to keep her occupied and absorbed during the day.

After work every evening, she raced home to search her mailbox for a letter from the selection committee. She recalled Mrs. Morgan's cautionary statement that either way the artists would be notified, so her excited anticipation mingled with a feeling of dread. *No news is good news,* she kept telling herself at the beginning of the second week.

She tried to brace herself for disappointment. Two nights a week she went to her night classes in design at the art institute. She was too shy to tell any of her fellow students that she had submitted sketches for the hospital mural. She had worked on those paintings at home. The sole person she had confided in was Molly Ellis, her only real family. Molly was a distant cousin with whom she had lived after her mother died and her step-father remarried.

An artist in her own right and a professional calligrapher, Molly had early recognized Joy's artistic talent and after her graduation from high school had encouraged her to apply to the art institute. She, more than anyone, understood what getting the commission for the mural would mean to Joy.

On Saturday Joy phoned Molly and spilled out her mixed emotions. "I'm afraid I want it too much, Molly," she said, recounting her doubts about her presentation to the selection committee, and her premonition that Dr. Wallace's objection to her theme would carry weight.

"Look at it this way, Joy: if it's in the Lord's plan for you, you'll get it. It's as simple as that. Remember, 'Be anxious for nothing, but in prayer and thanksgiving make your requests known.' That's all there is to it!"

"I wish I felt that confident," Joy said with a sigh.

"'Oh, ye of little faith'!" Molly admonished, laughing. To Molly, quoting Scripture came naturally.

"I know you're right, Molly, and I have dedicated my art to God. I want it to be an inspiration, to bring something special to people who see it. I remember how inspired I felt when John Feight spoke at the art institute. To use my talent for something as worthwhile as he does—painting beautiful, peaceful scenes to help people undergoing chemotherapy—that's what I thought about all the time I was planning my submission for the mural. To create something by which the families of patients in surgery would be uplifted, to give them hope in the possibility of mira-cles—" Joy paused. "Now I'm worried that maybe Dr. Wallace's comment will influence the rest of the committee against my idea. You never know how important one person's opinion can be."

"Joy, I know how much you've set your heart on this, but if it doesn't work out, try to remember that when one door closes, another opens."

"I'll try, Molly," Joy said. She hung up, wishing her faith was that strong and simple. It was what gave Molly her serenity. Joy had to work at her own.

A few days later, after a particularly hard day at work, Joy got off the bus at her stop and walked a few blocks further on the tree-lined street of older homes. This had once been an elite residential section of the city, but now most of the mansions had been turned into apartments.

When Joy had first come to the city, she had shared a room at the YWCA while she searched for an apartment where she could paint. Rents were mostly too high for her income. Through a series of strange coincidences Joy found her present home. Actually, it was a water tower.

It was on an old estate whose acreage over the years had been shrunk by subdivision and development. The ownership and destiny of the main house, a huge, many-roomed structure built in the twenties by a man and woman who entertained frequently, was in question. The water tower had been converted to create a hideaway to which the couple could escape when they had too many houseguests. The estate was now tangled in some kind of family litigation. The settlement of the case was pending, awaiting the location of several heirs. The final resolution could be tied up indefinitely. Evidently, no one else had thought the water tower a desirable dwelling place, so Joy had jumped at the very reduced rent.

Located just past the entrance to the property, at the beginning of the long, curving drive up to the house, the water tower was built on three levels and rose up surrounded by arching oak trees. The storybook architecture appealed to Joy's whimsical nature, and she had never felt convenience to be of particular importance

27

in choosing the perfect place to live. There was an outside stair-case that circled up to the first level, which contained a tiny living-dining room and a pocket-size kitchen. On the second level a small bedroom and a tiny bathroom were tucked under the eaves.

It was the third level that had sold Joy on renting the place. It seems that the wife of the original owner had been an ama-teur artist and had used the top room for a studio. It had a sky-light and a tile floor so that paint spills could easily be cleaned.

Joy, who believed nothing happened by chance, had come to consider the "tree house" meant for her. Tonight she was especially looking forward to its cozy refuge as she plodded wearily up the steps.

When she unlocked her door and reached inside to flick on the light switch, she almost missed seeing the long, white enve-lope marked "Special Delivery" slipped under the front door. She picked it up, saw that the return address was Good Samaritan Hospital. With suddenly shaky hands, she ripped open the flap and unfolded the letter inside.

Dear Miss Montrose:

The mural selection committee of Good Samaritan Hospital is pleased to inform you that you have been awarded the commission ...

She got no further before letting out an excited "Yay! Yay!" Spontaneously she did a thumbs-up high-step as she'd seen football players on TV do when they successfully complete a touchdown. She danced all around the tiny apartment and finally settled down to dial Molly's phone number.

"Oh, Molly, this means I can go to Europe to study art! They're paying me enough so I can really go! All my dreams are coming true!"

Evidently, Dr. Wallace's objection to her theme had been overridden by the rest of the committee.

chapter

4

THE FIRST DAY at Good Samaritan reminded Joy of her first day at school, a mixture of excitement and trepidation. Now that she had the commission for the mural, the full extent of what that involved began to hit her. There was so much preparatory work to do before she could begin the actual painting.

The sketches she had submitted for her presentation had been based on drawings she had made of friends, on studies in life classes at the art institute, and on photographs in her files. For the mural panels she would need live models. Where she would go about getting them she wasn't sure.

How would she find the right models for each of the stories she wanted to illustrate? Professional models would have to be paid. Some might object to coming into a hospital atmosphere. The hospital might object to having nonessential people on the surgical floor, where life-and-death situations were the order of the day. She was sure the hospital administrators wanted the work-in-progress to be as unobtrusive, as nondisruptive to routine, as possible. As Joy turned this problem over in her mind and worried about how she could manage this, she had an idea. An inspiration, actually. Why not use people right on the scene as models? Surely she could find the faces, the figures, the types she was looking for among the staff, the patients, the helpers, the volunteers. They might be willing—even flattered to be asked—to become part of the mural.

Since her first stop that morning was to check in at Dr. Fonteyne's office, she decided to run the idea by his secretary, Sylvia Thornton, ask her if she thought the chief of staff would have any objection to her plan.

"Why don't you ask him yourself?" was Sylvia's answer. She buzzed Dr. Fonteyne on the intercom. "Miss Montrose is here, Doctor. She'd like to speak to you if you have a minute."

To Joy's amazement, his response was enthusiastic.

"A splendid idea, Miss Montrose. It will make the mural a hospital project, get everyone personally involved. You certainly have my wholehearted approval."

Joy thanked him and assured him she would not interrupt anyone's work or get in the way.

From her desk Sylvia beamed. "If it matters, I think your plan would be great. The project has really sparked the staff's interest. We're all thrilled about your ideas for the mural, Miss Montrose."

Sylvia then informed her she would have to go to security to get her official name tag, which would permit her access within the hospital.

That accomplished, Joy came back on fourth and stopped at the nurses' station. She started to introduce herself and explain that she was there to measure the panels in the solarium, but did not get far. A tall, gorgeous redhead, whose uniform could not hide a stunning figure, smiled and said, "Oh, we know who you are. You're famous! An *artiste* in our midst! What can I do you for?"

"Well," Joy began, a little taken aback, "I just thought that since I'll be here every day, I ought to—" She paused. "Today I'm just going to measure the panels, figure out what basic paints I need, that kind of thing."

"No problem. I see you got your badge. Come on, I'll take you in and you can get started. Come and go, feel free. By the way, I'm Ginny Stratton." She opened the hinged half-door and came out from behind the counter and led the way down the corridor to the visitors' solarium.

On the way Ginny asked, "So how're you going about this?"

When Joy explained her plan to find models among the staff and patients, Ginny gave her a skeptical glance. "I don't think you're going to find any saints around here for your Bible panels."

"I'm not looking for saints, Ginny. Sometimes saints have the most unlikely appearances. Looks can be deceiving. Like in that old movie *The Portrait of Dorian Gray*. What I'm looking for are real people, just like the people Jesus dealt with. Real people to whom extraordinary things happened."

Ginny just nodded and made no comment. Joy got out her retractable tape measure and started measuring the spaces between the windows where the panels would go.

"Would you like a cup of coffee?" Ginny asked. "We have our own in the nurses' lounge—good stuff, not like the poison served in the cafeteria."

"Thanks, that sounds great." Joy went on measuring.

When Ginny came back, she brought two cinnamon buns along with two mugs of steaming coffee. They sat down to drink it. From her vantage point Joy had a good view of the elevator, and just then she watched it open and saw the young woman who had been on the selection committee emerge. Joy was curious about who she was and why she had served on such an influential body. Was she a doctor or an administrator or some other member of the staff? She wore no uniform but was dressed in a smart-looking pantsuit. As Joy watched, she stopped at the nurses' station and spoke to a couple of the

31

women there. There was a ripple of laughter at something she said. Joy turned to Ginny. "Who is that lady?"

Ginny glanced in the direction Joy was looking. "That's Sister Mary Hope. She's one of the chaplains. Works out of the pastoral care department."

"*Sister* Mary Hope. A *nun?*" Joy did a double take. The woman was about thirty, slim and attractive, with shiny brown hair stylishly cut. "She sure doesn't look like a nun."

"Aren't you the one who just said looks can be deceiving?" Ginny teased. "She was an airline flight attendant before she became a nun. All the things that made her good at that job make her right for this one. You ought to get to know her. I'm sure you'd like her. In fact,"—Ginny raised her eyebrows—"you two probably have a lot in common."

Joy had never been told she had nunlike qualities. But she let the remark go unchallenged. Ginny must have meant something else.

There wasn't time for more discussion about her, because Sister Mary Hope was coming toward the solarium. She greeted Joy with a radiant smile. "I'm so glad to see you. I was praying that your work would be chosen for the mural. It had a certain special quality about it that I noticed right away."

"Thank you." Joy felt her face grow warm with the sincerity of the compliment.

"Just wanted to welcome you to Good Samaritan and wish you good luck with the mural and God bless." Then with a wave of her hand she left.

"That was awfully nice of her, wasn't it?" Joy said, feeling humble.

"Sister Mary Hope's the greatest." Ginny jerked her head in the direction of the departing figure. "She visits with patients as well as their families. Sister Mary Hope is an expert in dealing with people's worries, problems, panic. Techniques she used to apply to the fear of flying now go to the fear of dying." Ginny laughed, then said, "Well, it's about time for doctors' rounds, and I'd better be at my post when they come in, especially Dr. Wallace." Ginny affected a deep shudder. "The ogre." With a wry smile she collected their mugs and paper napkins, saying, "See you around, Joy."

Joy spent the rest of the day measuring, making a list of supplies she would need, jotting down notes.

The following week she prepared the panel walls for painting. It was hard work and tedious. She had to fine sand, then apply two coats of primer, then add a neutral undercoat on which she could begin chalking in the background and figures.

From the beginning the project had enthusiastic support from the staff on the fourth floor, as well as from ambulatory patients and those in wheelchairs. Family and friends who were visiting stopped to ask about what she was doing.

From the very first day Joy searched for models. She found herself looking at people in an entirely different way, fitting faces to the biblical personalities she intended to use in the panels, searching for an extra quality. She felt like a casting director selecting characters for a play. Possibilities were everywhere, in the people she saw every day going about their work, in the ambulatory patients who roamed the halls or found their way to the deck just outside the solarium, or in the people in wheelchairs, hovering curiously a few feet away from where she was doing the primary painting. Joy always had her sketchbook at hand—ready, if the subject was willing, to make some sketches.

Almost every day Ginny joined her with coffee and sweet rolls, some juice, or a candy bar. "Found your models yet?" was her usual question.

"Not yet. Unless you want to pose?"

"*Me?*" Ginny exclaimed. "In a biblical role? Maybe the woman at the well," she said with some irony.

Joy glanced at Ginny. Evidently, Ginny knew her Bible.

Ginny caught the look of surprise and shrugged. "I was raised in a Christian home," she said nonchalantly, adding, "Not so you could tell it now. I mean, we practically lived in church. In the little town where I grew up, there wasn't much else to do. Twice on Sundays, and Wednesday night prayer meeting. When I went away to nurses' training was the first time I realized people did anything else."

Joy saw something pass over Ginny's face—an expression of sadness or regret?

Then Ginny quickly changed the subject. "Which panel are you going to do first?"

"I need a little girl, Jarius's daughter. I thought I could ask Dr. Braden if any of her patients are in the hospital."

Ginny frowned. "Well, you don't want one who looks too sick, do you? I mean, didn't Jesus raise her from the dead?" She paused before rushing on to suggest that Joy talk to the head nurse in pediatrics.

It was from Ginny that Joy learned that the hospital world was like a small town. Gossip circulated on a well-oiled "hot line." Ginny knew everyone and everything about most of the members of the staff. She had her dislikes as well as her favorites. Sister Mary Hope was one of her favorites. One day while Ginny was watching Joy work, she told her, "Patients who are depressed are her specialty. The newest medical methods, like drugs and painkillers, don't always work. That's where Sister Mary Hope and her pals come in."

"And does her method work?"

"Surprisingly, more often than not it does." Ginny raised her eyebrows. "Maybe I should try it myself."

"Don't tell me you are ever depressed?" Joy exclaimed, thinking anyone as pretty and self-assured as Ginny had nothing to be depressed about.

"If I were into self-diagnosis, I'd classify myself as close to being clinically depressed most of the time," Ginny commented dryly.

"You?"

"Yes, me." Ginny made a comic face. "Don't let this clown's mask fool you."

"But Ginny—," protested Joy, ready to go into her "power of positive thinking" mode.

"I don't want to disillusion you, honey," Ginny interrupted, "but I have plenty to be depressed about, if you only knew."

Whatever more Ginny might have said was interrupted by the PA system's page echoing down the hall: "Dr. Montrose, Dr. Gayle Montrose, please report to pediatrics."

Startled, Joy stood still, paintbrush in one hand, holding up her other hand to quiet Ginny. Joy tipped her head to one side, listening to the page again. Dr. *Montrose!* Her name. Not an everyday sort of name. If there was a doctor in this hospital with the same name, she would like to meet him.

"Listen, Ginny, they're paging a Dr. Montrose. Do you know who that is?"

"Yes, certainly. She's a pediatric oncologist. Just been here a few months."

"She? Dr. Montrose is a woman?" Joy was surprised and excited by this information.

"Yes, and very serious—all business. No kidding around. She's up here on fourth because one of her patients is being operated on. She'll be here all night if necessary. Totally dedicated." Ginny glanced at Joy. "Want her to pose for your mural?"

"Maybe. I don't know. She might be right for one of them. I can't tell until I meet her."

"She's quite beautiful, I think," Ginny said. "But I doubt if she'd consent to doing anything as frivolous—if you'll excuse the term—as being a model for a painting. Life is real, life is earnest for Dr. Montrose . . . and the grave is definitely *not* its goal. Her patients don't die, if she has anything to say about it."

chapter

5

A FEW DAYS AFTER Joy learned that there was a doctor at Good Samaritan Hospital who shared her name, Dr. Braden confirmed Ginny's comments about Dr. Montrose. Joy had gone down to the pediatric floor to study some of the children, searching for her Jarius's daughter. As she came out of the elevator, she encountered Dr. Braden. After an exchange of greetings, questions about the progress of the mural and about Joy's reason for coming to Dr. Braden's department, Joy asked her about Dr. Montrose.

"Gayle? She's wonderful. I've never seen a more devoted resident. She has no sense of time. Stays working until all hours. Goes the extra mile constantly for her patients." Dr. Braden halted, bit her lower lip as if considering whether to say more. "The only fault I find with her is that she absolutely refuses to acknowledge that anyone could die. Her patients must recover. A doctor eventually has to learn that in spite of all we can do, patients do die. Even children. And that of course is the hardest lesson of all, one Dr. Montrose has yet to accept."

Just then Dr. Braden looked past Joy and smiled, saying, "Here she comes now. I'll introduce you."

Joy turned in time to see a tall, willowy young woman walking toward them, wearing a long white lab coat. The fact that she was an African-American struck Joy only after her first impression of breathtaking beauty. Her skin was the color of creamed coffee, her black hair worn severely pulled back into a knot at the nape of a graceful neck. She had wide, dark eyes, a nose with slightly flared nostrils, and a full, curved mouth. She certainly fit Ginny's description. Dr. Montrose was striking in appearance.

When Jean introduced them, Joy thought she saw something curious flicker in Dr. Montrose's eyes. However, the woman paid close attention to Dr. Braden's explanation of why Joy was on their floor.

"Could you show Joy around?" Dr. Braden asked her. "Maybe even suggest a child for the panel she has in mind?"

Joy noticed a slight hesitation. Then Dr. Montrose said, "I'm just going off duty, Dr. Braden. Would tomorrow be all right?" She glanced at Joy.

"Of course. Any time that's suitable for you, Doctor," Joy said quickly.

"Fine. If you'll come down around ten tomorrow morning, I'll have made my rounds and then I'll be free."

Back on fourth Joy sought out Ginny and asked her to go to the cafeteria for coffee. As soon as they were seated, Joy asked, "Why didn't you tell me Dr. Montrose was black?"

"Why, would it have made a difference?" Ginny's lovely hazel eyes narrowed.

"No, I was just surprised. I guess I thought that with our having the same last name, she might be a long-lost relative. You see, I don't know anything about my relatives—at least my father's relatives."

Ginny's cup raised to her lips, halted. "Why not? Are you adopted?"

"No, but I never knew my father. He died before I was

born. He was a navy helicopter pilot and was killed in Vietnam. He and my mother met in San Diego when he was in training. They married there and then he went overseas. My mother was only a few months pregnant with me."

"Sorry. That must have been rough."

"Yes, on my mother of course. But she remarried when I was three, and we moved to Ohio. All I knew of my father was a photograph of him in his uniform. When my mother died when I was eleven, I found it among her things. I don't remember my mother talking about him. I guess she wanted me to think of Steve as my dad."

"And did you?"

Joy shook her head. "Not really. He was gone a lot, traveling in his work. Then after Mom died, I lived with some of his relatives for a while, then was sent to live with Molly Ellis, a distant cousin of my mother's. When my stepdad remarried, he just sort of dropped out of my life. Maybe it was my fault. I was a self-centered teenager—" Joy shrugged.

"I've got so many relations, I've lost count!" Ginny laughed. "So don't feel too bad, Joy. There's something to be said for being an orphan. Nobody to tell you what to do or what not to do, nobody to give you unsolicited advice or unwanted criticism. Most of my kin think I've gone wildly astray and don't mince words telling me so."

"It's funny, but hearing her name over the pager, then meeting her, made me realize how much I really have missed, not having a family. Maybe we do have some connection. I don't know, but I'd like to find out."

"Why don't you make a date to have lunch with her?" Ginny suggested. "Ask her about her family?"

"Dr. Braden asked her if she would escort me around pediatrics tomorrow. Maybe after that we could go have lunch or at least coffee."

"Good idea. But be careful. I believe she's a private sort of person. She might not appreciate you quizzing her," Ginny warned.

"Oh, I won't. I'll just tell her about me. I liked her. I'd like to get to know her."

Joy went back to work and worked steadily for most of the next two hours. All at once she felt very hungry and realized she hadn't taken time for lunch. When she stood up, she felt woozy and knew she had better eat something.

She took the elevator down to the lobby and found a vending machine. She pushed in her change, and a candy bar tumbled down into the little metal retainer. Then she got a soda from the soft drink dispenser next to it.

She had just unwrapped her candy bar and taken a bite with a sip of her cola when a stern voice behind her asked, "You know that stuff will kill you, don't you?"

Nearly choking, she whirled around. Dr. Wallace stood there, hands on his hips, glaring at her. He pointed to her candy bar and the soda can she was holding and shook his head. "That stuff knocks off laboratory rats by the dozens. You should take better care of your health."

Joy saw a twinkle in his eyes and a hint of a smile. She put on a hangdog look. "Caught in the act! I plead guilty. But there was no yogurt or granola in the vending machines. Maybe I should put in a demand for healthier snacks. Or is there such a thing as a suggestion box here?"

"I don't know. I'll bring it up at the next staff meeting," he promised. He remained there for a minute as though he wanted to say something else. "How's the mural coming along?"

"Well, I'm only doing the undercoating so far. But I think it will be fine—I hope so."

"Good." With a brisk nod he turned and headed for the elevator.

Joy looked after him. Those were the first words she'd exchanged with Dr. Wallace since she'd begun work at the hospital. She had seen him once or twice, striding purposefully from the O.R. or toward recovery, looking straight ahead. She had rather hoped to continue avoiding him, feeling that maybe he resented her because over his objections her theme had been approved for the mural.

However, he hadn't seemed that hostile or formidable just now. Joy recalled Ginny's reminder that appearances can be deceiving. Maybe she had been wrong about Dr. Wallace as well.

Joy's first two weeks at Good Samaritan had certainly been full of interesting meetings, unexpected encounters, and strange coincidences.

chapter
6

JOY WAS LOOKING FORWARD to Dr. Montrose's promised tour of pediatrics. The minute Joy stepped off the elevator, she was conscious of being in a different environment from that on the other floors. There was something in the air that was tangible, lighter somehow. Why should that be? The place was full of sick children, some of them seriously so. That's what Drs. Braden and Montrose dealt with every day.

Joy walked slowly down the corridor, past rooms where the doors were open. Nurses were busy adjusting IVs, administering medication. Most rooms had four beds. The walls were painted soft yellow and hung with colorful posters. Bunches of bright balloons floated from door frames, and the staff behind the nurses' station wore flowered smocks instead of uniforms. Joy looked down the hall into what appeared to be a large playroom. There children were gathered around a pretty young woman who was telling them a story, using hand puppets. Although the children wore bathrobes and of course no one was running about, shouting boisterously, the scene resembled a kindergarten. In spite of the fact that some of the children had IV poles dangling above their wheelchairs, and some little heads were bald from the effects of treatment, the atmosphere was cheerful.

At the far end of the corridor there was a waiting room. It looked much the same as those on the other floors. Chrome furniture with plastic cushions, a TV going with the sound turned low. A daytime soap was on, figures moving across the screen, carrying on a scripted dialogue. Yet the real events taking place in front of the set, where parents sat with anxious faces, haunted eyes, haggard expressions, were far more dramatic.

Joy turned away, feeling an intruder on others' grief. Some of these children were terminally ill. She had come down here to search the ward, look for a little girl she could use for Jarius's daughter. She recalled Ginny's caution about not wanting a child that looked "too sick."

Then through an open door Joy saw her. She was perfect. A sweet, round face framed with short blond curls. Joy felt that inner click she got when a subject was right, and knew she had found her model.

She went to the nurses' station to find out who the child was and to see if she could get the parents to agree to let her pose.

"You mean Debbie Matthews," the nurse on duty told her, reading from her chart. "But you'll have to get permission from her attending physician."

"Who is that?"

"Dr. Montrose."

Joy's first thought was, *Oh, good. I'll ask her today.* She was pleased that the search for her first model had been so easy. Then Joy recalled what Ginny had told her about Dr. Montrose, and wondered if it would be hard to get her permission. The doctor who dealt in life-and-death situations might think that posing for a mural would be a trivial, shallow thing for her patient to do.

She saw Dr. Montrose in the distance, standing at the door of a patient's room. It was the same door through which Joy had seen the little girl she thought would make an ideal Jarius's daughter. As Joy approached, Dr. Montrose saw her, greeted her with a nod. She then turned to the little girl sitting up in a bed decorated with several balloons.

"Debbie, here's someone I'd like you to meet. Her name is Joy." Turning to Joy, Dr. Montrose said, "Here is one of my favorite patients, Debbie Matthews."

Debbie gave Joy a long, appraising look over the heads of several enormous stuffed animals—a floppy-eared bunny, a teddy bear, a sad-eyed white baby seal. With one thin little hand she fingered the bunny's ears. Slowly her mouth curved up into a shy smile, and she said, "Joy's a pretty name."

"Joy's an artist, Debbie. Tomorrow after your chemo we'll take you upstairs so you can see what she's painting on the fourth floor."

"Chemo?" Debbie's voice echoed plaintively. "Do I have to have more needles stuck in me, Dr. Montrose?"

"'Fraid so, angel. But that's a piece of cake for you." Dr. Montrose turned to Joy and explained, "Debbie's been here twice before. She's a real trooper."

They said good-bye to Debbie and walked down the corridor together. Dr. Montrose told Joy that before she could show her around further, she needed to stop at the nurses' station to make some notes on patients' charts. "I'm sorry; it will only take a minute," she added.

"Actually, I've already looked around quite a bit on my own," Joy responded. "But if you have the time, I would love to talk with you over coffee."

"Well then, why don't I meet you in the cafeteria after I finish my rounds?"

Joy was eager to ask Dr. Montrose if she could use Debbie as her model. She waited at the entrance to the cafeteria until the doctor joined her.

"Sorry I'm late. Something came up just as I was leaving. What was it you wanted to talk to me about?"

When Joy explained, Dr. Montrose didn't answer right away. Instead she took her time pouring each of them a cup of coffee. When they had seated themselves at a table, Joy prompted, "So? What do you think?"

"Why?" Dr. Montrose asked. "Why Debbie?"

"She's a beautiful child. Those eyes, those ringlets. She'd be perfect."

"You know her prognosis is terminal," Dr. Montrose said flatly. "I've seen the latest tests. They show it's just a matter of time." Her face was impassive as she continued. "Leukemia. A virulent type. But maybe we can beat those odds. Each time we send her home, we hope. But then each remission period is shorter. We keep trying . . ." Her mouth settled into a grim line.

The enormity of what she said kept Joy silent.

"I'm sorry," she said finally. "She would have made such a beautiful Jarius's daughter. Those curls—"

"She'll lose her hair . . . the chemo," Dr. Montrose said shortly.

"Oh, Gayle, that makes me so sad." Joy had inadvertently used the woman's first name.

Neither of them spoke for a few minutes. Then Joy had a thought. "If her parents give their permission . . . I can show them my sketches, tell them how a painting of Debbie would be a lasting memorial to their little girl . . . no matter what happens. And I think it would make her happy during whatever time she has left. Couldn't she come up in her wheelchair sometimes and watch me paint? Wouldn't that be a good thing, Gayle?"

Gayle stirred her coffee thoughtfully for a few seconds, then said, "I think she's strong enough to pose for a few sessions, if you like."

"Really?"

"Yes. But you'd better get started soon. Before her curls are gone," Gayle said dryly.

During the next two weeks the painting of Jarius's daughter went well. Gayle had only approved twenty minutes of posing time with a break every five. Joy worked faster than usual. She loved the time she spent with the little girl. Debbie was thrilled at the idea that her picture would be painted on the wall.

Joy brought her the book *The Velveteen Rabbit,* one of her own favorite childhood stories, to read while she worked. Debbie loved it, too. At nine she could read very well and took to reading out loud as Joy sketched.

The unexpected bonus to choosing Debbie as her model was that Joy and Gayle became friends. They often had lunch together after leaving the ward. Although Joy didn't ask her directly, Gayle began to tell Joy about herself. Because of Ginny's warning, Joy refrained from discussing the coincidence of their identical last names. Instead she asked Gayle how she had decided to become a doctor specializing in children's cancer. "That seems such a hard specialty to have chosen."

"No branch of medicine is easy. I guess you could call it a calling. I believe I was by nature called to work with children, sick children. There's so much possibility with children, that they will get better, will recover. I don't know. Don't you ask yourself how you became an artist? I think all of us have a plan for our lives. The main thing is to find it, recognize it as yours, and go for it."

"So it isn't so much that you chose it but that it chose you?"

Gayle paused, looked at Joy for a long moment as if deciding whether Joy would understand the next thing she was going to say. "Get real, Joy. A black woman doctor. God has something to do with it. A whole lot. None of this has been an accident. It was tough for me to get into medical school, tougher to stay there. There is a reason for all this. One that I didn't plan. My interest in medicine, to begin with. Nothing in my background, in our family, could have predicted this. Yet I always knew that somehow—I didn't know how—it was all going to happen.

"It was all hard work. And even when I graduated, became an intern, it all seemed like some kind of dream." Gayle stopped and laughed, a full, rich laugh. Then with a quick raising of her eyebrows she added, "Or maybe I should say more like a nightmare. Still, I couldn't believe it. I'd catch a glimpse of my reflection in a window or mirror, in that white jacket with the name tag that said, 'Gayle Montrose, M.D.,' and I'd think, *That's not me. That's somebody else.*"

Joy wasn't sure just how, but one day while they were talking about the mural, Dr. Evan Wallace was mentioned.

"Oh, him." There was something dismissing in Gayle's tone. "Surgeons have it easy, if you ask me. They're free from patients' pain. They don't have to know they're hurting someone; they don't see them grimace or hear them moan. Their patients are anesthetized."

"Don't you like Dr. Wallace?"

"I don't *dislike* him," Gayle countered. "It's just that he is like so many surgeons—cold, aloof." Gayle frowned. "It's their attitude. Such control, such confidence—" She paused. "But maybe that's the way they have to be. Maybe it's how we all *should* be. What they warned us about in medical school—not to become emotionally involved with your patients. Surgeons, as I said, have an advantage over other doctors on that."

"Isn't that helpful? I mean, to do what they have to do? They have to be sure—it's not a guessing game."

Gayle's eyes widened and Joy quickly amended her statement. "Not that that's what other doctors do, but isn't diagnosing a

kind of, well, trying one thing, then something else, sort of . . . ,"
she finished weakly, hoping she hadn't offended Gayle.

"I wouldn't say that," Gayle said slowly. "You do have to
test, check symptoms, compare, narrow it down to one thing
or another . . . experiment," she conceded. Then she smiled.
"Hey, this conversation is getting way too serious, too philo-
sophical. I've been meaning to ask you, would you like to
come to my apartment for dinner? My next night off is
Thursday."

Thrilled to be invited, Joy immediately accepted.

"Shall I bring something?"

"No, of course not. You might not guess, but cooking is my
hobby. Having a guest gives me a chance to show off," Gayle
said with a laugh.

Joy was early. She waited on the balcony outside number
10, and in a few minutes she saw Gayle's Corvette pull into
the parking lot below. As Gayle got out of the car, she looked
up, saw Joy, and waved.

Gayle came up the stairway carrying a huge bunch of golden
chrysanthemums. Under her arm was a paper sack from which
the top of a long loaf of French bread emerged. When she
reached Joy outside her apartment door, she apologized. "I'm
sorry I'm late. I stopped to get a few things, then saw these in
a flower stand and couldn't resist. I had to find a parking place,
then go back and buy them. You know, 'hyacinths for the
soul.'"

Gayle juggled her packages and handbag, got out her keys,
unlocked the door. "Come on in," she said over her shoulder,
and Joy followed her inside.

"What do you mean, 'hyacinths for the soul'?"

Gayle looked surprised. "Don't you know? Haven't you ever
heard of it?"

Joy shook her head.

"Well, the poet called the Guilistan of Moslih Eddin Saadi, a Mohammedan sheik, some seven hundred years ago wrote this:

> If of thy mortal goods thou art bereft
> And from thy slender store two loaves alone to thee are left
> Sell one, and with the dole
> Buy hyacinths to feed thy soul.

"It's my rule of life. Even when I was a miserably poor student, I practiced it. Now, when I'm a miserably paid resident, I still practice it," she said, laughing.

"I love it! I'm going to copy that down, give it to Molly to write in calligraphy for me, then frame it and put it up in my apartment and begin to practice it," declared Joy.

Gayle gave her a long, steady look. "But you *do* already, Joy. I don't know anyone who is more appreciative of life than you. You were certainly well named."

"Why, thank you, Gayle." Joy felt herself blush. Coming from Gayle, that meant a great deal.

"Make yourself comfortable. I'll go fix us some tea," Gayle told her and went behind a bookcase divider into the small kitchen.

Joy looked around. Gayle's apartment was like its occupant, she decided—spare, neat, tasteful. There was a large sofa covered in a rough textured linen, a russet leather Eeams lounger and hassock, a Boston rocker. In one alcove she saw a desk of pale wood, on which was a computer monitor, a study lamp. The place had a restful, uncluttered atmosphere that Joy found refreshing.

Over the angled fireplace hung a painting. Joy went over to examine it.

There was something familiar about it, not the scene so much as the style, the brush strokes, the composition . . . a landscape in autumn, a country road overhung with trees, bordered by Queen Anne's lace, purple wild asters, a rustic fence. Bending closer, she read the artist's signature.

"Gayle!" she called. "Where did you get this painting?"

Gayle came to the arch between the living room and kitchen, teakettle in one hand. "Oh, that! In a small New York gallery. It was my present to myself when I graduated from medical school. I worked a deal with the gallery owners. Had them put it away for me. Paid for it on the installment plan after I'd paid off my student loans," she said with a laugh. "It took a long time . . . but it was worth it."

Joy turned slowly around, staring at her.

Gayle frowned. "What's the matter? Don't you like it?"

"Gayle, the artist. Jeff Montrose. He was my great-great-grandfather."

Gayle took a few steps into the room, stood beside Joy in front of the painting. She bent closer, squinting to read the tiny signature in the right-hand corner of the painting. "I never even noticed it. I just loved the painting. Something in me responded to it for some reason." She turned and looked at Joy. "Do you suppose . . . ? What do you know about this Jeff Montrose?"

"Nothing more than what Molly told me. When I lived with her when I was in high school, she said my artistic ability was probably inherited. She said my mother had told her that one of my father's relatives had been a famous artist. That's all."

"This is some kind of coincidence, isn't it?"

The two young women looked at each other wonderingly.

51

chapter
7

"JARIUS'S LITTLE DAUGHTER" was well under way. Joy had utilized the time well and was excited and pleased with the results. The little girl, Debbie, was so pretty. Ironically, she seemed the picture of health, at least to Joy. Her bones were delicate, her features dainty, and her skin had a lovely translucence that made her lovely to paint. Was this a sign of her fragile health? Joy hoped not. There had been blood transfusions, she knew. She would have to ask Gayle if the child was improving.

All this was on her mind one afternoon when she was absorbed in her work painting the scene that, as she imagined it, would be visible through the bedroom window of Jarius's child. She had become used to the hospital atmosphere. It seemed almost to provide her with a concentration she needed. She could turn off the constant hum of activity, the sound of the wheels of food and medicine carts on the linoleum floors, the muted footsteps of interns and nurses and staff, the steady beep of pagers, the buzz of phones—all became the background of her daily work.

Suddenly a long shadow fell across the panel. Startled, she turned to find Dr. Wallace standing behind her. Joy felt her face grow warm. How long had he been standing there watching her?

As she looked up at him, she thought again what a marvelous face his would be to paint. It was a tense face, the muscles under the tan skin taut, the mouth resolute, in the eyes . . . an unfathomable depth. There was strength and character in that face.

"How's it going?" he asked.

"Good," she replied. "It's only in the first stages."

She examined her brush, then moved as if to turn back to her work, but his next words stopped her.

"I owe you an apology, Miss Montrose."

Surprised, she turned back toward him. "You don't owe me anything, Dr. Wallace."

"Yes, I do," he said stiffly, then paused. "May I buy you a cup of coffee in the cafeteria?"

Further surprised at this unexpected invitation, she shook her head. "Thank you, but I'm working."

"You've been working steadily since I came on the floor, since I finished rounds. You need a break, and I need to explain." His voice had the hint of an order, the kind he was used to giving and having others promptly obey.

She glanced at him and realized he was not going to take no for an answer. "All right."

She took time to clean her brush meticulously and put it back in its plastic holder, then unbuttoned her paint-smeared smock and tossed it on a nearby chrome chair. She rolled down her shirtsleeves, gave her hair an ineffectual pat.

A brief smile touched the corners of his mouth. "You look fine."

Joy felt annoyed that her unconscious gesture seemed to imply that she gave an importance to her appearance at his invitation. She wished she had not accepted it, but Dr. Wallace was already waiting for her at the solarium door. There was nothing to do but join him.

As they passed the nurses' station, Joy was aware of curious glances following them. She could just imagine the ones which might be exchanged once they stepped inside the elevator and the door closed behind them.

Downstairs Joy was once again aware of the curious glances from fourth-floor staff members who were in the cafeteria as they entered together and made their way from the coffee dispenser to a booth.

Dr. Wallace placed one of the mugs on the Formica top in front of her, then slid into the seat across from her. He took a sip, made a face, then grinned.

"Should have remembered how strong this stuff is at this time of day," he murmured. "Shall I get you something else? Tea? Juice?"

"No, it's fine. I've grown used to this hospital brand by this time. Although I must say, the coffee in the nurses' lounge is much better. Ginny Stratton brings me some from there. They've got the formula down pat."

Dr. Wallace pushed his mug aside, folded his hands, and leaned forward on his elbows.

"Now, about that apology I owe you. After your presentation we—all of us on the selection committee—spent a great deal of time studying your submissions." He halted. "You are quite good, you know. But there was more—and we all noted it—aside from the professional skill. There was a quality, something no one could define, that cast the deciding vote. I didn't see that at first. That's what I wanted to apologize about. I'm sorry."

His words hung suspended, as if he wanted to say more but did not know how.

Joy was taken completely off guard. She had never expected such an admission from the doctor. At the same time, she was again struck by the artistic appeal of his face. Without being

"Greek god" handsome, he was enormously attractive. Everything about him was so clean, so defined—the shape of his nose, the determined chin, well-shaped mouth. She looked at his hands. Hands told so much about a person. Evan Wallace's were no exception. Strong, the fingers long, tapering, hands made for performing the delicate operations for which he was so highly known and praised.

Her attention was brought back to what he was saying.

"We also went to the Bradens' office and looked at the mural you painted there." A smile tugged at his mouth again. "It was amazing. You almost made me believe in fairy tales."

Joy laughed. "Then maybe *this* mural will make you believe in miracles!"

At her remark Dr. Wallace's expression subtly changed. He stared down into his coffee mug, then back at her with a strange, almost wistful look. "I'm afraid I don't believe in miracles, have that kind of faith . . . " He shrugged.

"Well, there's hope," Joy said softly, somewhat taken aback by his blunt admission.

"I'm afraid I'm not very big on hope either," he said crisply.

Joy almost asked, "What about love?" but stopped herself. Instead she said, "I should think that, as a doctor, you would feel that hope was important. Necessary in fact for a patient to recover."

He shrugged. "Hope? Well, a positive mental outlook is at least beneficial. However, I don't believe in offering false hope to my patients. I tell them what the facts of the surgery are, the potential risks as well as the possible results. I just don't believe in miracles."

There was an awkward pause. Then Joy tried again. "Is that why you objected to my theme for the mural?"

A frown deepened the furrow between his eyebrows. "Does it matter? Obviously, I was outvoted. Besides, personal considerations should not have entered into the decision. Your work won the day." He changed the subject abruptly. "There's something I'm curious about. Something I noticed on all your sketches. That little bee beside your name at the bottom right. Does it have any significance?"

"Yes, actually it does." Joy hesitated, then said shyly, "But if you don't believe in miracles, I don't know how to explain it."

"Try me."

"It's very personal to me. When I first came to the city, my goal was to attend the art institute, but I only had enough money to last me a few weeks. I had to find some kind of job. It was scary, to say the least. But Molly—she's a kind of relative of mine—kept telling me to have faith, to believe that God had a plan for my life, a purpose for giving me my talent and the desire to develop it." Joy's voice faltered a little. However, Dr. Wallace was listening intently, and even though she was unsure of how he would react, she had gone this far and had to continue. "Living expenses were much higher than I'd anticipated. Time was running out. I still hadn't found work and only had another week's rent at the YWCA. Everything seemed pretty impossible. I called Molly in tears, and she reminded me that with God nothing is impossible."

Joy's hands tightened around the coffee mug, and she took a long breath. "I kept telling myself that, and then I did have a miracle. Two days later I got a job and a partial scholarship to the art institute. That's where I heard John Feight, and"— she opened both her hands, palms up—"now you know why I believe in miracles."

"That still doesn't answer my question," Dr. Wallace said persistently. "Please explain the bee."

"Oh, the bee. Well, aeronautically speaking, the way the honeybee is constructed, it's impossible for it to fly. At least there's no scientific explanation for it. Impossible, see? But it *does*."

She looked at him. He was frowning fiercely. No telling what he must have been thinking. She finished limply, "I guess I identify with the honeybee."

He seemed to be turning that over in his mind.

"Surely you can understand the principle," she said. "It must have taken *you* a great deal of hard work, sacrifice—whether you call it that or not—to become a surgeon."

"Hard work, sacrifice, yes! I don't know about faith. The truth is, it came at a high price. To someone else the cost was great." His mouth twisted slightly, and there was a bitter edge to his statement. Whether he would have explained that terse remark, Joy never knew, because at that moment his electronic pager sounded.

He cut it off. "Sorry, I have to go. I have two patients in post-op." He stood up, looked down at her, and said, "This has been a very interesting conversation, Miss Montrose. We must do it again another time."

Then he was gone. Joy sat there sipping her coffee, wondering if she had said too much, revealed too much about herself.

It was hard to tell what Dr. Wallace was thinking. He was a hard man to understand. Yet there was something about him . . . What was it? Slowly it dawned on her. The recognition she felt was not because they had met before; rather it was that she had seen him in her creative imagination. His face was exactly the sort of face she had envisioned for the centurion in her mural, the Roman officer who had come to Jesus begging for healing for a servant. The same features—the steely eyes, the controlled face. His body was also that of a highly disciplined athlete.

The only thing missing was emotion. Wouldn't the centurion's face betray his distress over the illness of his favorite servant? Presumably, the physicians had given up. Why else would this proud Roman officer seek a Jewish healer for help? The man had risked his reputation among his fellow officers, among his own men, to come to Jesus. Wouldn't he have had some anxiety about that?

Dr. Wallace's face was carefully controlled. Would anything move or touch him deeply enough so she could portray his feelings in a painting?

The possibility mingled with doubt. Dr. Wallace would never consent to pose. Especially when he had so adamantly declared that he did not believe in miracles. Could she dare ask him? Could she risk it?

chapter
8

THE PANEL OF Jarius's daughter was finished and received favorable comments from the staff. Debbie Matthew's parents were especially pleased with it.

Joy still had four empty panels waiting to be filled and so far had not found models for them. When she had prepared her initial presentation, Joy had had no trouble envisioning each panel, but now choosing the right models was another thing altogether. Finding the right people to pose for the mural had become a fascinating detective game for Joy.

Armed with her sketchbook, she roamed the corridors of the hospital as nonchalantly as possible while searching for faces for the paralytic, the blind man, the centurion's servant, and Peter's mother-in-law.

One day she was wandering around the first-floor lobby, wondering if she might have to look among the visitors for a model for one of the panels. She went into the hospital's gift shop, which was run by the hospital's volunteer auxiliary, and there behind the counter Joy spotted a woman who might just be right for Peter's mother-in-law.

Joy hung around, trying not to look conspicuous as she studied her. Had Peter's mother-in-law been old or simply middle-aged? Joy knew that women in biblical times married young, in their teens. By the time they were thirty, they had grown children, probably married ones; some women were even grandmothers in their forties.

The lady behind the counter was perhaps in her mid-forties, possibly her early fifties. She was very attractive, her silvered dark hair perfectly set, her makeup skillfully applied, giving her olive skin a richness and her brown eyes brilliance. Although her nose was quite long and her mouth wide, she had a lovely smile. From her vantage point by the greeting card pyramid, Joy watched her as she graciously dealt with an indecisive customer.

Joy hesitated. Maybe she was too theatrical looking. But on the other hand, she would make a striking subject. Joy moved closer to get an even better look. The plastic name card pinned to the lapel of the woman's pink jacket read, "Mrs. Moira Andrews." Joy lingered indecisively, trying to act as though she were idly searching for a get-well card.

"May I help you?" a soft voice asked. Joy turned to find the subject of her artistic scrutiny at her elbow.

"Are you looking for a card for someone special?"

"No . . . I mean, I . . . well, actually, I was . . ." Joy halted, and then said, "I'm Joy Montrose. I'm painting the mural in the solarium on fourth, and—"

"Of course. I'm delighted to meet you. The auxiliary was totally enthusiastic about the idea when it was brought before the board. I've meant to come up and see how it's progressing, but I somehow get stuck in the shop on days I work here." She lowered her voice. "Sometimes it's mostly browsers, people who are at loose ends, waiting for a family member to get out of chemo or surgery—or just killing time." She winced. "How I *do* hate that expression, don't you? As if time isn't the most precious thing we have. I've become very conscious of that, volunteering here two days a week." She paused. "Is there any way I can help you?"

Joy plunged right in. "Truthfully, Mrs. Andrews, I was looking for a model for one of the panels I'm planning, and I was wondering if you would consent to pose for me?"

Mrs. Andrews looked surprised. *"Me?* Pose? I don't know . . ." She flushed. "What would it involve? I mean, in time? You see, my week is pretty much filled—I come here two days a week, then Wednesday is my garden club, and Friday I play bridge . . ." Her voice trailed off hesitantly. "I really don't know."

Quickly Joy explained her method of working. A few informal sketching sessions until she got the angle she wanted, then a few hours of positioning her figure in the overall composition.

"I suppose I could arrange it, shift some things around. My hairdresser appointment could be moved . . . ," Mrs. Andrews began. While they were talking, two people had come into the shop. One was now standing at the counter with a stuffed elephant in hand, waiting to pay for it.

Mrs. Andrews glanced over her shoulder, then touched Joy's arm and whispered, "Excuse me, my dear. Customers. Let me think about it and let you know." She hurried away.

Joy realized that Moira Andrews' face was the kind she longed to paint. The bone structure was good; the eyes particularly held depth. The few visible lines around them and around her mouth could be accentuated in the portrayal of Peter's mother-in-law, a woman whom Joy imagined had seen much of life—joy, sorrow, loss, pain, troubles of many kinds. Joy guessed that in spite of the fact that Moira Andrews was perfectly groomed, expertly made up, she too had known some deep valleys. If only Joy could portray that. She felt an excitement, as she always did when she was on the edge of creating. She hoped she could persuade Moira Andrews to become a model.

Back on fourth, Joy worked on the background of the panel she intended to use for the healing of the paralytic. She outlined temple pillars and the distant blue of the Judean hills. She was concentrating so hard that at first she didn't hear her name being spoken. It was repeated—"Miss Montrose." Joy stopped painting and turned, brush in hand, to see Mrs. Andrews.

"I don't mean to disturb you, but I just came up to see your work. The painting of the little girl is lovely, so lifelike. You are a very talented young woman." She looked at Joy for a moment. "And you're so young—how old are you, dear?"

"Twenty-three."

Moira shook her beautifully coifed hair. "About the same age as—" She paused, then said quickly, "I've decided I'd like to pose for you—that is, if you still want me to."

"Oh, I'm so glad, Mrs. Andrews."

They arranged a day and a time for her to come. Mrs. Andrews took out a small notebook and a pen and jotted it down. "Oh dear, that's my bridge day. But no, this is much more worthwhile. I'll get a substitute," she said with a firm nod, replacing her notebook and pen into her purse. "I'm so glad you asked me. Peter's mother-in-law. Hmm—I don't think I even knew Peter was married or had a mother-in-law. I guess I have some catching up to do on my Bible reading. Well, thanks again. I'll see you on Wednesday."

Mrs. Andrews gave Joy a little wave of her hand and left the solarium, her high heels making small tapping sounds as she walked down the hall toward the elevator.

The second week Moira Andrews was posing for Joy, she said with the breathless air of one sharing a great confidence, "You may be interested to know, I bought a New Testament and started reading it."

Joy halted, brush poised, to look at her with surprise.

"I'm not proud of it, but I confess I'd never really read it before. Not really. Oh, I was familiar with some of the most quoted verses and with some of the Psalms, like the Twenty-third. Of course we had a Bible in our house, prominently displayed on our bookshelf. You know, one of those showy red leather ones with gold lettering. But I'm ashamed to say that although I dusted it regularly, I rarely opened it."

Joy made no comment, just went back to carefully painting in the detail of the veil Moira was wearing. It was an Indian sari that Moira had suggested herself. She had brought, for Joy to choose from, several she had purchased when she was on a trip to India a few years ago. Originally she had bought them to wear as a fashion statement to some of the large parties she and her executive husband attended. Joy was unsure at first of using one. Then she decided that the way it draped was artistic, and she had painted a linenlike texture to substitute for the gauzy gold material, and it had turned out fine.

"I read a chapter or two before coming here on the days I pose," Moira continued. "In fact, other days too. It's a very interesting way to start my day. I wish I'd done it years ago when . . ."

Whatever else she was going to say was lost in a deep sigh.

Joy painted on, letting the silence lengthen. Beyond the solarium, the regular hospital noises went on—an orderly pushing a laundry cart went by whistling, a doctor was being paged, elevator doors opened and shut.

Joy took a few steps back from the panel, tipped her head, and surveyed critically what she had done.

"Well, that's all I need, Mrs. Andrews. I like to let a painting mellow. Then I can come back, fill in more details later. You've been very patient, and I really appreciate your doing this. I know it hasn't been easy for you, switching all your appointments around the way you had to."

"No, you're wrong, Joy. It's I who should thank you. Posing for you, spending these quiet hours with you here in the solarium, has given me time to think, time I never allowed myself before—because it was too painful. I've made such a mess of things—my life, the lives of those dear to me. I've been a foolish woman. Too often I've let pride govern my decisions. I've made so many mistakes that have hurt others. I thank you for this time. The tapes you played while I was posing—some of that music I would never have listened to before. Sitting there, I had to listen, and the words began to make sense to me . . ."

To Joy's dismay, Mrs. Andrews began to cry. Tears rolled down unchecked, sending narrow rivulets of mascara down her cheeks. She sniffled, groped for a handkerchief. Joy stood by helplessly, not knowing quite what to do. Here was a woman who had everything—wealth, beauty, status in the community—and she was weeping like a brokenhearted child.

"You see, Joy, I have lost something very precious, and I don't know if I can get it back . . ." She wiped her eyes and began to talk. "I have a daughter. I never mentioned her to you because we've been estranged now for nearly three years. It's my fault. She was our only child, and we lavished her with everything—at least we thought we had. My husband was wealthy, so we were able to give her everything—toys, a pony. And we always took her with us on vacations—cruises, Bermuda, skiing in Aspen. We sent her to the best schools, gave her a beautiful debut, a coming-out party at my husband's country club, and then . . ."

The tears started coming again. Impatiently Mrs. Andrews dabbed at her eyes. "Then she came to tell us she'd fallen in love—and that's when it happened. The young man was totally unsuitable. No education to speak of, no profession—in fact, he was a commercial fisherman! Came from a family of fishermen—father, brother, grandfather. I told her they had nothing in common, that she would regret it if she were foolish enough to marry—"

Moira stopped to blow her nose, and Joy wondered how she could not see the irony in what she was telling her about her daughter's choice. Moira took a deep breath and went on. "I influenced her father to stand with me—against the young man, against the marriage. I refused to even see him or to meet his family. I carried on terribly, Joy—I see that now. In the end she regretfully, reluctantly chose him over us. After all we'd done for her . . ." Moira broke down again. "At first she tried. She sent letters, cards, but we—at least I—returned them. I didn't allow my husband to relent—weaken, I called it. I kept saying she'd be back once she realized that we were right, that a marriage like that couldn't work, that it wouldn't last."

Moira drew a long, sighing breath. "We haven't seen or heard anything for months. I don't even know how to reach her, to tell her I'm sorry, ask her to forgive me . . . I'm sure her husband resents us. Things were so bitter, such harsh things were said, that I don't think it will ever be forgotten. A reconciliation seems impossible. It would take a miracle."

Joy reached out and took Moira's hand, gently pressing it. "That's what these panels are all about, Mrs. Andrews—miracles. Let's ask Jesus to perform a miracle. Let's ask him to restore your relationship with your daughter. That kind of miracle is just as important as the physical healings."

It had taken a kind of boldness Joy didn't know she had, but Moira Andrews had seemed so desperate, so needy, that Joy had been filled with compassion. It struck her that Jesus was often so filled with compassion for the desperate people to whom he ministered that his caution had been overcome and he had prayed for their healing, knowing that his heavenly Father would honor that prayer. In a way Joy had felt that, too.

She had been very aware of Moira's need at that moment and had lost her self-consciousness.

The way Moira hugged her before she left warmed Joy's heart. Moira had initially seemed to be so contained, so reserved, so in control. To see her like this, open and transparent, allowing her emotions to be revealed, was startling—a miracle in itself, actually. Healing could take place. Joy was sure of it.

The solarium opened out onto a large circular deck where on clear days ambulatory patients and those in wheelchairs could go to enjoy the fresh air and sunshine. Some of them usually stopped to say a few words to Joy or just watch quietly as she painted. Joy became used to this and overcame both her reluctance to work with an audience and her feeling that she had to open a conversation. If questions were asked, she answered but did not initiate further exchange.

One of the more frequent spectators was a man who regularly took advantage of the mild weather and came every morning when the sun was at its peak. He had first been wheeled out to the deck by one of the aides, then gradually had progressed to a walker. He was in his fifties, with gray hair and strong features. He was tall and well built, although with his present disability he had to lean heavily on the chrome walker, his massive shoulders bent forward.

After pausing a few times at a short distance from her, then moving on, he began to linger. Joy acknowledged his presence with a smile, then went back to her painting. There was, however, something about his face that drew her. One morning, taking longer than usual to clean her brushes, she studied him. There was an expression that seemed strangely vulnerable.

As he realized she had stopped work momentarily, he moved slowly forward. "Very nice, young lady," he said.

"Thank you," she said, smiling.

"I don't mean to appear ignorant, nor am I any art critic—in fact, I have to admit I know next to nothing about art. To tell you the truth, I was never much interested—never had the time, actually—but I'm guessing this has some kind of central theme?" He looked at her inquiringly. "These people in the painting, the shafts of light you're placing them in—I don't really get the significance . . ."

"Each of the panels represents one of the healing miracles of Jesus," Joy told him.

Immediately she saw his eyes narrow, his cheek muscles twitch slightly. He nodded. "Oh, it's a kind of religious thing."

"Well, you could call it that," Joy said slowly. "But I like to think of it more as a symbol of hope, the light of faith . . ."

"Hmm, I see," he said in a noncommittal manner. "Well, I'll go along now, leave you to your painting, young lady."

Joy watched him make his halting way back into the corridor and down the hall. Who was he? It seemed curious that he didn't make the connection of the panels. Was it possible that a man of his age and obvious intelligence did not know about the healing ministry of Jesus?

When she left to take her lunch break, she stopped at the nurses' station and asked who the patient was. Aris Domingo was on duty and took one of the physicians' charts out of the bin near her desk and checked.

"That's Mr. Kenan, Philip Kenan. Dr. Wallace's patient. He's recovering from hip replacement surgery." She looked up at Joy. "Why did you want to know?"

"He has a wonderful face—deep-set eyes, furrows in his cheeks, jutting jaw!" She laughed. "I'm always looking at faces as models, you know."

Aris affected a pose. "How about a beautiful Latino for one of the panels?" She rolled her eyes dramatically. "I would like to be immortalized on the walls of this hospital!"

Joy laughed again. "I'll see what I can do."

Aris's pretty face became suddenly serious.

"I feel sorry for the guy. He never has any visitors. He checked himself in the day before he was scheduled for surgery. No one came to wait during his operation, nobody called about his condition, no flowers, no cards, and as I said, no visitors since." She shook her head. "He's got a private room and is staying here to recover. Weird. Most patients are eager to go home as soon as their doctor will discharge them. But Mr. Kenan seems perfectly content to stay on." Aris shrugged. "Maybe he has no one or nothing to go home to."

Joy couldn't get Philip Kenan out of her mind as she worked. Aris's thumbnail sketch of him kept nagging at her. She was also intrigued by the complex face, a mixture of strength and . . . and . . . what? Sadness? Loneliness? He was seemingly a man without family or friends.

The conviction grew that she could use him to good effect in one of the remaining panels. Which one? The centurion? No, too old. The Roman officer would be young, vigorous, muscular. Joy knew who she *really* wanted for that character. But Mr. Kenan might be right for the paralytic, the man who was lowered on a stretcher by his friends into the house where Jesus was healing. However, Philip Kenan had no friends. Somehow that struck Joy as the saddest thing about him. How would he feel about being asked to pose? Would he be insulted? She recalled the look that had come over his face when she explained the theme of the mural. Was it hostile, angry, puzzled, or was there something of longing and loss in it?

Joy determined that the next time Philip Kenan stopped when she was working, she would engage him in conversation, try to find out more about him, tactfully suggest that he model for her. Would he be offended? There was only one way to find out.

"Still here?" a voice demanded. "You keep long hours."

Joy recognized Dr. Wallace's voice and turned. "I'm just quitting," she told him. "Speaking of long hours, you're here late, aren't you?"

"I had a patient in recovery, wanted to check on him after he regained consciousness," he said shortly. "Have you eaten, or are you still ignoring medical advice and living on candy bars and soda pop?"

Joy laughed but his remark reminded her that she hadn't had anything but the bagel and coffee Ginny had brought her before she went off duty hours ago.

"No, guilty again."

"What about getting a bite with me?" came the surprising suggestion.

"In the cafeteria?"

"Not likely. I know a great little place not far from the hospital that serves the best lasagna."

As Joy hesitated, Dr. Wallace said, "You have to eat."

Joy glanced around the solarium and saw that the light coming through the tall windows was fast fading. She *was* hungry and she did love Italian food. Besides, if she was eventually going to ask Dr. Wallace to pose for her, maybe this was a good way to get to know him better. Perhaps then she could ask him to be her model for the centurion.

As if assured she would accept, Dr. Wallace glanced at his wristwatch. "I'll change and meet you in the lobby in ten minutes, okay?"

She nodded and watched him walk away. Then Joy cleaned her brushes, put away her paints, and took off her smock. After freshening up, she passed the nurses' station on her way to the elevator. As she said good-night to the staff on the night shift, she wondered with some amusement what they would say if they knew she was meeting the aloof Dr. Wallace downstairs.

He was waiting right by the elevator when she got off, as if impatient for her arrival. As they crossed the lobby toward the doors leading outside, he asked, "How is the mural going?"

"Good, I think. I've got quite a bit more to do on the characters, though. By the way, I'm hoping to get a patient of yours to pose for me. Mr. Philip Kenan."

"Ah yes, Kenan." Dr. Wallace frowned. "I doubt if you can convince him. But then, I suppose I should never underestimate an artist's persistence. Mr. Kenan has nothing else to do. I wish you luck."

Joy thought it would take more than luck. Another miracle.

In the parking lot Dr. Wallace walked briskly to the space reserved for physicians and unlocked the door to the passenger side of a gleaming red Porsche. Joy slid into the smooth leather seat, thinking it was quite a contrast to the lumpy seat of her old clunker.

The restaurant Dr. Wallace had recommended lived up to his description. It turned out to be a charming, unpretentious place with round tables and bentwood chairs, filled with family groups. The two of them entered and were greeted by the sounds of laughter and lively conversation, the spicy smells of Italian food, and a warm welcome from a plump, smiling, dark-eyed woman who greeted Dr. Wallace by name.

He introduced Joy. "This young lady is a talented artist, Mrs. Regli. She's painting a mural at the hospital."

"It's good to see the doctor not eating alone tonight," the woman said, smiling at Joy as she showed them to a table. "Not good for the digestion to eat by yourself." She snapped her fingers, and a young waiter came to take their order.

When the waiter left, Dr. Wallace turned to Joy and said, "So tell me, how did you get into mural work in the first place?" He leaned forward, apparently quite interested.

"At the art institute," she replied. "A guest speaker, John Feight, inspired me."

"Never heard of him. A famous artist?"

"Yes. He's a businessman, and also an artist, a poet, who got this idea of brightening the hours of cancer patients receiving radiation treatments, by painting beautiful scenes on the ceilings of treatment rooms. As you certainly know, patients have to be alone while they're being treated, and it can be a lonely, depressing experience. He began in a Georgetown oncology department, and since then he's painted in hospitals all over the country. He's been an inspiration to other artists, who are now doing similar work. I volunteered with some of them at a local clinic, which is where I met Dr. Braden. When she first saw my work, she asked me to paint a mural in her pediatrics office."

Dr. Wallace was regarding her so intently that Joy began to feel uncomfortable. Then he said, "I envy you your talent."

"But you have a talent, too. You're a brilliant surgeon. Everyone at Good Samaritan says so."

He made a dismissing gesture with his hand. "Technical skills are not art."

"I disagree. I think surgery is an art. It's up here, isn't it?" Joy tapped her forehead. "You have to see it in your mind, your imagination, before you can do it. It's the same with painting. You visualize the scene, and then you try to put it down as you saw it. It takes skill, yes, and concentration, and more than anything else, the desire to do it well. That's a talent."

Dr. Wallace smiled. "I never thought about it like that. You've given me something to consider, Miss Montrose."

Just then their waiter brought their food and set down their plates with a flourish. Afterward their conversation turned to lighter things, and Joy was surprised to find that Dr. Wallace had several other interests besides medicine. Music, for instance.

After they left the restaurant and were back in the car, he slipped a cassette into the tape player, and the interior was filled with the sound of Beethoven's Fifth Symphony.

"I have season tickets to the community concert series. Perhaps sometime you'd like to attend a concert with me," he said.

She was so surprised that she could only murmur something that sounded like, "That would be nice." It still seemed incredible to her that she was with Dr. Wallace and seeing an entirely new side of him.

"Where to? What's your address?" he asked as they moved onto the street.

"Back to the hospital parking lot. I left my car there."

They covered the few blocks rapidly and pulled into Dr. Wallace's space. Joy started to get out, saying, "Thank you very much, Dr. Wallace. You were right—that was the best lasagna I've ever tasted."

"Wait, where are you parked?"

"Not far. I have a temporary parking permit for the staff parking lot."

"Well, I'll walk you to your car," he said.

"That's not necessary," Joy protested, but he was already getting out of the car.

As they crossed the parking lot, two of the fourth-floor nurses coming off shift exited the hospital building and saw them. From the shocked look on both women's faces, Joy knew that the fact that she and Dr. Wallace had been seen together would be topic A at tomorrow's coffee klatch.

"Good evening, Dr. Wallace," the two nurses said in unison.

"Good evening," he responded curtly.

When they reached Joy's car, he chuckled. "Well, that will provide some grist for the mill, won't it? Oh, I know what they say about me behind my back. Cold fish. No social life. Well,

74

this will give them something to talk about. I hope you don't mind being linked with me as an item."

Joy laughed. "I don't think it will come to that."

He helped her into her car and waited until she had backed out and turned. She tapped her horn lightly, then drove off, leaving him standing in the empty space, watching her leave.

chapter

9

CONTRARY TO DR. WALLACE'S prediction, Philip Kenan agreed to pose for Joy. In fact, he seemed flattered when she approached him with the idea.

To Joy's immense pleasure, Mr. Kenan turned out to be an interesting raconteur. He told her about his nomadic early life as a kid of fifteen during the Depression. He regaled her with stories of his days spent hitchhiking across the country, riding in boxcars with out-of-work hoboes, earning money as a jack-of-all-trades, taking any kind of employment he could get.

He posed for her several times, but Joy was having difficulty painting his face. Not the features but the expression. The paralytic should have a look of hopeful expectation; Philip Kenan's face remained stoic, closed. Twice she wiped out what she had done and started over. There was something missing that she knew was there if she could only capture it.

Mr. Kenan was in no hurry. He seemed, in a strange way, to enjoy the posing sessions. Joy recalled Aris's comment: *"Maybe he has no one, nothing to go home to."* Joy promised herself to ask him a question that might draw out some information, some emotion she could use in painting the paralytic's face.

But it wasn't until they were nearly finished with the portrait that Philip Kenan told Joy the most important story of his life. One day he asked her, "You're religious, am I right, young lady?"

"Well, if you mean am I a believer, Mr. Kenan, I most certainly am. Religious—I'm not sure exactly what that means."

"You're a Bible reader, right?" He pointed to her Bible beside her paint box.

"Yes, sir," Joy answered, wondering where all this was leading.

"So was my mother," Mr. Kenan said in a husky voice. "My mother died when I was a small boy. But I remember going to sleep at night hearing her singing . . . hymns, it must have been. 'What a Friend We Have in Jesus,' 'How Great Thou Art.' I think they must have somehow sunk into my child's consciousness. But after her death my father and I lived a kind of roustabout life. He was in heavy construction, and we went wherever his jobs were. Sometimes he dumped me off with some relatives—never for very long, a few months of a school year—then he'd pick me up again and I'd go with him to the next site. We lived in motels or a company-owned trailer on the site. I was left alone a lot—but always on the fringe of the life he had with the other men. There wasn't much religion in it. So I grew up with only the faintest memory of my mother's beliefs. I was a smart kid, though, and when I was fifteen I had a teacher, someone who really took me under his wing and showed me that education was my way out of my father's rootless lifestyle.

"I don't blame him, though. I'm sure he did the best he could, having been left with a little kid when he was still a very young man, and he made our living the only way he knew how. But what I'm saying is, I didn't have what they'd call today a role model—that is, until this teacher came along. Mr. Emmons. To make a long story short, he showed me I had brains and how to use them. So I told my dad I wanted to stay and finish high school, then go on to college, if I could get in.

"That's where Mr. Emmons again helped. I got a scholarship to the state university. I had to work for room and board, but I did get through and graduate. Then I got a good job—" Mr. Kenan stopped. He was leaning forward, hands clasped in front of him, pressed together. The knuckles were white. "Well, I guess you could say I had it all. The job, moving up on the ladder they call success, steadily getting ahead . . . I married, acquired the whole bit—the house in the suburbs, a summer cabin on the lake, two swell children . . ." He drew a long, ragged breath. "Then I blew it. I didn't know I was blowing it. I was too concentrated on me. I thought it was for them. But my wife got tired of playing second fiddle to my ambition. She got tired of all the moving. You see, I picked up this restlessness from my dad—there was always a better job, a company willing to pay more. I didn't care about neighbors, my kids' friends, their team, or my wife loving a certain house, her friends, her place in the community . . . I never had time for any of those things." He threw out his hands in a gesture of resignation—or was it helplessness? Joy couldn't be sure. She was listening intently.

"We got the divorce; she got everything. In a way, I was trying to make up for what she said I hadn't given her in the marriage. As a result of the divorce, over the years I've lost contact with my children. I thought it was better to stay out of their new lives. I kept supporting them of course; I didn't abandon my responsibilities. Then my wife remarried, and my kids . . ." His voice trailed off. "Anyway, that's the story. I'm fifty-seven years old, and I've accomplished everything I set out to do, but—"

Mentally Joy finished his sentence for him. *"What does it profit a man if he gain the whole world and lose his eternal soul?"* She felt sorry and sad for Mr. Kenan with his empty life. And she felt true sympathy for his needs. How could she help? How to assuage the deep regret, the sorrow he felt, the suffering of broken dreams, of a misspent life?

"There's always a second chance, Mr. Kenan. Maybe if your children knew how you felt, things could be patched up. I don't think it's ever too late."

Mr. Kenan's eyes looked bleary, but he said gruffly, "You're young, Miss Montrose." He paused, then added, "Done for today, are we?"

"Yes, and thank you very much for posing for me."

"Thank you, young lady. I'm being discharged tomorrow. They won't let me goldbrick any longer. That's what Dr. Wallace told me. Got to go someplace where they will supervise my physical therapy, get me walking again."

"I hope everything goes well for you, Mr. Kenan. And you must be sure to come back when the mural is finished, see how it all turns out."

Mr. Kenan nodded and without another word left the solarium, the walker thumping as he shoved it along.

As Joy cleaned up and put her things away, she thought over the day's session. It was becoming more and more apparent that the mural was a ministry—something she had never dreamed it would be. People were being healed. Emotionally, Moira Andrews, and now, hopefully, Philip Kenan. Something had truly happened to them while they stood in the shoes of the people whom Jesus had healed. She thought of the sign over the altar in the little church she attended when she visited Molly: "Jesus is the same, yesterday, today, and tomorrow."

It was true—she was a witness to that.

It was the very next day that, while working from sketches and her memory of Mr. Kenan's expression when he was talking about his losses, Joy finally caught the look she wanted in the paralytic's face.

chapter
10

ONE MORNING A FEW days later Joy's old car refused to start. She had to call a tow truck to take it to the garage. There the mechanic shook his head skeptically and gave her the bad news that it might be the transmission. Not wanting to think about what that would involve and how much it would cost, Joy asked him to call her with an estimate. In the meantime she had to take the bus to the hospital.

During the day she was adding to some of the backgrounds of the panels, finishing some details. She became so totally engrossed in her work that she almost forgot she would have to catch a bus home. After checking the schedule she had picked up that morning, she realized she would have to leave right away, since she had to walk quite a few blocks to the bus stop on the corner.

She was just hurrying out the entrance when Dr. Wallace caught up with her. "Leaving early for a change?" he asked.

"My car's in the repair shop, so I've a bus to catch," she explained.

"Let me drive you home," he suggested as they walked out the lobby door together.

"Thank you, but I don't want to put you to the trouble."

"Nonsense. No problem," he said decisively as he took her elbow and led her toward the physicians' parking lot.

Joy knew it was useless to argue and couldn't help but be grateful. Her car trouble that morning had been the beginning of a long, frustrating day in which she was plagued with a nagging concern about repair costs. It would be nice to sit comfortably in the luxurious car and be driven right to her doorstep.

"I see you got Philip Kenan to pose for you," Dr. Wallace commented as they drove out of the hospital entrance.

"Actually, I think he enjoyed it."

"He did seem to be in better spirits when I discharged him. Did you have anything to do with that?" He glanced at Joy with a slight smile.

"We talked, or rather *he* talked, I listened. I think his life is pretty empty now. But he had an interesting one. He told me all about his adventures as a young man."

"I think you have a talent for bringing people out of themselves, Miss Montrose."

"I don't know about that, but I did like him very much. I told him to be sure to come back when the mural is completed, and he said he would—" She suddenly broke off, gesturing. "Turn here at the next intersection."

Dr. Wallace read the sign. "Oakhurst. That's a prestigious old neighborhood for a struggling young artist, isn't it? If I remember correctly, this used to be where all the grand old mansions were, once upon a time."

" 'Were' is correct. Most have been torn down or made into apartments. I rent a small place on a family estate that is tangled in a legal dispute. It's temporary until that gets settled." She pointed. "There's the entrance. You can drop me off just inside the gate."

When he pulled to a stop, Joy suddenly felt she ought to offer him some hospitality, since he had been kind enough to bring her home. He didn't seem in any rush to be anywhere. "Would you like a cup of tea or coffee?" she asked.

"Sure, very much," he said, adding in a teasing tone, "I'd like to see what kind of environment a creature like you inhabits."

"Come along, then," Joy said. "Follow me."

Dr. Wallace got out of the car and stood for a minute looking rather puzzled. "Where?" They were standing under a huge old oak tree, and he looked up through the leaf-laden limbs. "A tree house?"

"A water tower."

He shook his head. "Leave it to an artist to fall in love with the most improbable living quarters."

"Wait until you see it," she said with mock severity. "It's perfect, exactly right for an artist."

The approach was along a brick walkway under a trellised arch with espaliered grapevines overhead, to a twisting outdoor staircase that led up to the small deck. Joy ran lightly ahead of Dr. Wallace and then unlocked the door and stood waiting for him.

"Welcome," she said, smiling.

The front door opened into a small room with a pint-size kitchen off one side and a dining alcove nestled in the opposite corner, with windows looking out onto the leafy upper branches of the tree. There was a small circular stairway leading to the next level. "My bedroom, bathroom, and studio are up there."

"Very nice, very cozy, very like you," Dr. Wallace said, glancing around at the wicker furniture, the bright, flowered chintz pillows.

"Would you like some herbal tea?"

"Yes, thank you. I think that would be most appropriate to have while visiting this kind of fanciful abode," he teased. His whimsical sense of humor amused her and would, she knew, also surprise the nurses on fourth if they knew about it. Joy realized she was being allowed to see a side of Dr. Evan Wallace that he rarely showed to other people. Why, she wondered, did he feel comfortable enough to show it to her?

While she busied herself behind the counter that separated the sitting room from the kitchen, Evan walked around the small space, taking in everything. He went over to the bookcase, which had been improvised of boards and cement blocks, and checked out the titles. There were among the art books all kinds of children's picture books.

He pulled out a large one, *The Velveteen Rabbit*. Holding it flat open in both hands, he turned the pages carefully, stopping here and there to read.

Seeing him, Joy leaned over the counter. "Aren't the illustrations fantastic? I buy children's books when I admire the pictures. But that story is especially wonderful. For grown-ups, very powerful." She paused. "The little girl who posed for Jarius's daughter loved it, too. I brought it for her to read, to keep her amused."

Evan put the book back on the shelf as Joy brought a tray with a teapot and cups and set it down on the table in the windowed alcove.

As she poured the aromatic, steaming liquid into cups and handed him one, Dr. Wallace asked, "By the way, tell me again—who is Molly? A relative, right? You've mentioned the name several times. She seems to be someone important in your life."

"Oh, she is. Very. She is family, although we're only distantly related. After my mother died and my stepfather remarried, I lived with Molly. She's an artist, too. A professional calligrapher. Does all sorts of things, like diplomas, award citations, invitations for special events. She was the one who encouraged me to try for the mural commission."

Dr. Wallace nodded. "It's always important, maybe even necessary, to have one person who believes in you."

Joy detected a note of sadness in his voice, as if somehow that had been missing in his life. But he quickly redirected their conversation, giving her no chance to pursue the subject. "Thanks for inviting me up here. I appreciate you're allowing me a glimpse into your private world. I find you fascinating, Miss Montrose."

"Me, fascinating? No one has ever told me that before." She laughed. "Strange maybe or a little weird or"—she affected a French accent—"a wee bit too *artistique?*"

"Not at all. I think you're quite delightful."

Joy felt warmth rise in her cheeks under his speculative gaze. "So how goes the progress on the mural?"

"Three panels are nearly completed, except for some detailing and the glazes that I'll apply when I'm finished," Joy told him.

"They really look good," he said.

Dr. Wallace expressed interest in hearing more about her work on the project, and Joy was happy to share her thoughts and feelings about the process of taking her vision and making it into a reality. When their conversation turned to the centurion panel, it was the perfect opening for Joy to ask him to consider posing, but somehow she couldn't bring herself to do so. Before she could gather enough courage, Dr. Wallace changed the subject and her opportunity was lost. Eventually he finished his tea, stood up, and said he must leave.

As he walked to the door, he stopped to look at the picture hanging in an alcove of the living room. It was of Christ standing in a dark garden, holding a lantern in one hand and knocking on a door with the other.

"This is interesting," he said. "Is it by one of the old masters?"

"It's a reproduction of the famous painting *Light of the World* by Holman Hunt, one of the Pre-Raphaelite painters." Joy came over to stand beside him as he examined the picture. "There's quite a story behind the picture. The artist started working on it at night in the dead of winter in an orchard. He insisted on painting in the actual setting he wanted to use. After it was exhibited at the Royal Academy in 1853, it was sold to Thomas Combe of Oxford, whose wife later presented it to Keble College. To me, one of the most remarkable things about the original painting is the amount of detail, considering its small size. Later Hunt painted a second, much larger, version which now hangs in St. Paul's Cathedral in London."

"That's strange," he murmured. "Despite all the detail, there's no handle on the door."

"That's exactly what the critics said when it was unveiled for the first time."

"Why is that?" Dr. Wallace asked.

"The artist explained that it was an illustration from the Scripture verse in Revelation that reads, 'Behold, I stand at the door and knock; if anyone hears and listens to and heeds my voice and opens the door, I will come in to him and will eat with him and he shall eat with me.' The door represented the human heart, and that can only be opened from the inside."

Dr. Wallace nodded but said nothing. When he turned to look at Joy, his eyes were reflective.

"Someday I'm going to see the original," Joy told him. "It's in London."

"Is that one of your dreams?"

"A longtime dream, but when the mural is finished, I think I'll have enough money to go."

"It's good to have dreams, even if they don't all come true," Dr. Wallace said, and again Joy thought she detected a tinge of sadness in his voice.

At the door he turned back, then said, "I had a dream. To have a cabin in the hills, someplace I could go, a sort of retreat where I could do a little fishing . . . I did accomplish part of it but not the whole dream." He hesitated. "It's about a two-hour drive from here, and the woods are beautiful just now with all the fall colors. I wonder—would you like to drive up there with me on Saturday? It would be an artist's paradise. You could bring your sketchbook and paints. I have a few winterizing jobs I should do at the cabin, and you'd be free to do whatever you'd like."

Surprised, Joy hesitated. Again she was struck by the opportunity to get to know Dr. Wallace better, have a better chance of getting him to be the model of the centurion in her panel. "Why, yes, thank you. I'd like to very much."

"Great. We'll get an early start so we can have the best part of the day up there. I'll bring a picnic lunch." Dr. Wallace's face was transformed with a wide smile.

"Thank you, Dr. Wallace."

He frowned. "Can't we make that Evan—outside the hospital?"

"Yes," she said, smiling. "Why not? And you can call me Joy."

chapter
11

SATURDAY MORNING THE SKY was a bright and cloudless blue. When Joy opened her door to Evan's knock, she saw he was wearing faded jeans, worn boots. He looked young, almost boyish.

"Ready?" he asked with an eager smile.

"All set." Joy slung her canvas tote bag containing sketchbook, watercolor pens, some brushes over her shoulder. As they went down the steps, Joy saw a yellow jeep. "Where's the Porsche?"

"Need a vehicle with four-wheel drive to get up to the cabin. It's a pretty steep, narrow road."

"Just how many vehicles do you own?"

"Three. I use a pickup most of the time to haul things up there or bring brush or firewood down. But"—Evan grinned as he opened the jeep's door for her to get in—"it's in no shape to drive a lady around in. I just use it for heavy duty, not pleasure."

It was not long before they were leaving the expressway and starting up into the hills, which were ablaze with early autumn color. The scenery was so beautiful that Joy was totally absorbed. They finally turned off the two-way highway onto a road, not much wider than a logging road. As they rounded a hairpin bend, Joy got her first glimpse of Evan's "cabin in the hills." Instead of the rustic shack a man might use to store tackle and some basic staples for an occasional fishing trip, Joy saw a well-crafted log-and-stone house with a slanting roof supporting solar panels, and a large deck that circled the whole building.

She looked over at Evan curiously. "I thought you said this was a cabin. It looks like a picture out of a posh resort brochure. Is this what you call roughing it?"

"It started out small and just kept getting larger." His smile faded and his mouth firmed. "Actually, coming up here and working on it was therapy."

Joy gazed up at the house. "This is really elegant. I had no idea . . ." She turned to him, teasing. "So this is how the other half lives, Dr. Wallace?"

"Correction—*Evan*, remember? We agreed that outside the hospital, first names," Evan said, then added, "Wait until you see the view."

Joy followed Evan up the steps to the deck and looked in the direction he pointed. Spread out before her was a magnificent panorama of rolling blue hills with blazes of crimson, gold, and bronze against the darker green of pines and cedars. "It's gorgeous," she murmured.

"What did I tell you? Get out your paint box, do your thing. I've got plenty to keep me busy."

He went back to the vehicle to retrieve a toolbox and a wicker hamper, which he held up. "Lunch, whenever you're ready."

"You think of everything, don't you?"

"Boy Scout training. Be prepared."

Evan had unlocked the door into the house, and Joy went inside to get water. She glanced around. The interior was all paneled in gleaming redwood. The furniture was scarce and rather stark. There was a built-in counter and high stools in front of an L-shaped kitchen. Stairs led up to a loft. The cabin had an unused feel, and Joy wondered how often Evan came up here and if he was always alone.

She got her water and went back out on the deck, where there were two Adirondack chairs and a table on which she put her supplies. She propped her watercolor board against her knees and wet the first sheet of paper with a wash of water. She could hear the sound of a hammer in the background; gradually it faded as she became so caught up in her painting. Soon she was not aware of anything but the beauty surrounding her, the crystal-clear mountain air, and the pure joy of creating.

"Okay, lunchtime." Evan's voice broke her reverie as he came up on the deck carrying the wicker hamper. He opened it and spread a blue woven cloth on the table, set out several plastic containers.

"Don't tell me you whipped all this up by yourself?" Joy asked, setting down her watercolor board and sketchbook.

"No, can't take any credit. Remone's Deli is responsible. I'm a regular customer."

"And a valued one, I suspect. Will you look at all this!" Joy exclaimed. "Pretty fancy, I'd say. Not the kind of picnic I'm used to."

"Nor am I. When I was an intern, I lived on a diet of canned baked beans, peanut butter, and bananas. But I'm trying to get used to this."

"The affluent life?"

"Believe what you will about doctors, but most of us didn't start out that way. Me, for instance. I grew up in a small coalmining town in Kentucky. My grandfather and his father before him were miners. The only way my dad got out was that he played football and got a scholarship to the state college. He became a high school teacher. Taught all his life. Was determined that none of his sons would go down in the mines. But affluent is not what I'm used to, not by a long shot." Evan handed her a plate. "Help yourself. Coffee later."

Evan took his plate and set it on the wide arm of the Adirondack chair.

"So then what did you do? I mean, to become a doctor?"

"Worked like a dog to earn my way through pre-med," he said shortly. Joy got the impression that Evan didn't want to talk more about his past, so she changed the subject.

When they finished eating, she leaned her head back against the chair and sighed, saying, "This is marvelous."

"Come, I'll show you something even more spectacular. A place where on a clear day you can see three states." Evan took Joy's hand and pulled her to her feet. Still holding her hand, he led her down the deck steps, behind the cabin, and out along a trail covered with pine needles. They climbed a winding path to the top of the hill. There they sat down on a sun-warmed rock. The view was breathtaking. The valley was vivid with autumn foliage; the silver slash of the lake glittered between rocky ridges; and over all hung a smoky blue haze.

"This is so lovely and peaceful," Joy said in a hushed voice. "If I had a place like this, I'd stay here forever."

"That was sort of my plan. At one time I thought of just chucking everything, coming up here and living."

"In a way, that would be a waste for you, Evan. You have so much to give. Your skills as a surgeon are so valuable. So many people's lives depend on your expertise."

"Well, solitude isn't all that good if your mind and soul aren't at peace. Being alone just accentuates whatever is troubling you. You have no way to work it off." A smile touched his mouth. "Of course, most Good Samaritan staff members think I vent my frustration over personal problems on my residents, the interns, and nurses. 'Ivan the Terrible of O.R.'"

"No way, Evan. All I hear is how much they all admire you."

"Well, they probably wouldn't say anything bad about me to you, Joy."

She didn't know how to answer that, so she just let it go.

By the time they returned to the cabin, it was late afternoon, and Evan said they should probably start packing up to leave. "I hate to see this day end," he added, frowning, "but you can't hang on to happiness. That's one thing I've learned."

Impulsively Joy asked, "Why are you so bitter, Evan?"

For a minute Joy thought he wasn't going to answer, that he was angry at her for asking. He put his toolbox and the picnic hamper in the back of the jeep, then faced her.

"I hadn't planned to talk about this. At least not yet, anyhow. Maybe this is as good a time as any. Let's have some coffee." He took out the thermos and poured them both full mugs, then led her over to the deck and they sat down on the steps.

"You know I was married," he began. "I don't talk about it much. Not to anyone. But I want to tell you, Joy. I want to tell you about Susan.

"We were married when I was an intern. She had just graduated from nurses' training. We'd known each other in high school, gone together to school events. We weren't particularly romantic about each other—good friends, mainly. Both serious about our careers. Later our feelings changed. We realized we loved each other, were each other's best friends, which is a good basis for marriage."

Evan took a long swallow of his coffee before continuing.

"In spite of the odds, we decided to get married. Susan was working as an RN. If we had waited, it would have been seven years before I was through, years before I could start a practice. Susan was more than willing to support us. We had no idea what marriage under those circumstances would really be like. It was very hard—a grind, actually. I was studying night and day. We hardly saw each other, because she was working different shifts."

Evan shook his head. "I don't think I appreciated how hard it really was on Susan. Finally, the summer I finished my residency and before I began two years of surgical residency, we decided to take a vacation. Our first one." Again Evan shook his head, as if in disbelief. "We planned a two-week camping and backpacking trip. Susan loved the outdoors as much as I did, so we went up to the Sierra-Nevada wilderness area." Evan clenched his hands and took a long breath, as if what he was about to say was painful.

"We were miles from anywhere. Susan developed flu-like symptoms and became very sick. I wanted to start back but she wouldn't hear of it. She said that it was probably a twenty-four-hour virus of some kind, that she'd just stay in her sleeping bag and rest, that she'd soon be fine. She urged me to go on, to hike further in to a little lake we'd heard was full of trout, and to just let her sleep. So I did. I was gone most of the day, and when I got back early evening, Susan had a raging fever. I knew right away it was serious and blamed my stupidity for not insisting we start back earlier. By the next morning she was delirious, and I knew we were in big trouble. I carried her back to where we'd left the car. It was quite an ordeal. She was a big girl and now she was a dead weight, limp with fever. We were both strong climbers. On the way up we hadn't minded the rocky, steep path. I got her to the car, and even then in my panic I think I knew it was too late. By the time we got to the nearest hospital in a small mountain town, she had lapsed into an irreversible coma. The diagnosis was bacterial meningitis, the kind that strikes suddenly and is deadly. Even in the best conditions its symptoms are easily confused with those of any number of other illnesses. Without sophisticated testing, it's impossible to know how to treat it. Anyway, it was already too late."

Evan's face became a mask of resentment. "It was so unfair.

94

We were only in our mid-twenties. Susan had made it possible for me to become a doctor, to go on with my plans, and she never had a chance to reap any of the rewards. She never got to enjoy any of the benefits, the prestige of my position, the material perks—nothing," he said fiercely. "Now maybe you can understand why I'm low on faith. Susan was such a good person—kind, generous. That's why I find it hard to believe in a personal God who cares about individuals."

"I'm sorry, Evan," was all Joy could think to say.

"That was six years ago. I was in pretty bad shape for a while after Susan died. Then I threw myself into my work. To prove somehow that all her sacrifice had been worthwhile. For the next five years I didn't do much else but work. I got a chance to join the staff at Good Samaritan, and it helped. I thought being in a new place, among people I didn't know and who didn't know me, would help me get a new outlook, allow me to get on with my life. Lately, however, I see that work isn't enough. I've narrowed my life too much. Susan was practical, sensible, levelheaded. She wouldn't have been happy about the way I've handled my life since her death."

A rueful smile tugged at his mouth as he looked at Joy. "But I do think I'm beginning to change. I'm reaching out more. I can see other possibilities for my life, my future. I'm ready now to take on life again—a whole life." He took a long breath, then stood up. "I just thought you deserved to know that you've helped me do that. You also needed to know what I was coming out of. . . . I wanted to tell you. I didn't want any shadows hovering . . ."

The day was fading into a purple dusk when they drove in under the huge oak tree near Joy's little house.

Evan turned off the motor and said, "This has been a special day, Joy, thanks to you."

"I enjoyed it, too. Thanks for a lovely time," Joy said and got out of the car. "See you Monday at the hospital."

As Evan drove off, Joy realized that all of her former awe of Dr. Wallace had vanished. She saw him now not as the formidable surgeon but as a vulnerable human being with his own struggles. She found she liked the man she was getting to know.

chapter
12

AFTER THAT SATURDAY at the cabin, Evan became—without Joy being fully aware of it—more and more a part of her life. Almost every day, he stopped by the solarium and they took coffee breaks together. Often on Sundays, after Joy had been to church, they met somewhere for brunch. Sometimes Evan came to the art museum when Joy researched costumes and backgrounds, and they had lunch in the restaurant there. In fact, it wasn't long before being together on the weekends during which Evan was not on call seemed natural.

Joy was not even aware how much time they spent together, until one day during a conversation with Ginny, the nurse asked in her blunt way, "So what's with you and the Iceman?"

Joy blinked. "What do you mean?"

"I'm not criticizing, just curious. And I guess I envy you a little. Cliff and I can't be seen together openly. No theater, no restaurant, no event. As the song goes, 'We meet in the shadows, afraid to be heard . . .'"

Joy knew of Ginny's affair with a married doctor; it was one of those open secrets no one at the hospital was supposed to know about but everyone seemed to.

"I still don't know what you mean, Ginny."

"Oh come on, Joy. Don't you realize that you and Dr. Wallace are doing the kinds of things together that people in love do? You'd have to be blind not to see the way he looks at you."

It came as a shock that they had been not only observed but speculated about.

That conversation with Ginny startled Joy into thinking about how much time she was spending with Evan. Ginny had once confided to Joy that she often had to alter her plans to fit in with Cliff's schedule or accept a last-minute invitation from him, and Joy realized that she was now doing the same. Just last week she had skipped her evening class to go to a local revival of the Broadway musical *South Pacific*. It was a dangerous parallel to Ginny's situation. Joy could see how easy it would be to become attracted to someone, put that person's demands ahead of her own goals. The thought of letting anything interfere with her dream of going to Europe, visiting the galleries and museums of the Old World, seeing the great art masterpieces firsthand, was frightening. She couldn't let anything change that long-held plan.

Joy planned to spend the long Thanksgiving weekend with Molly, who lived about sixty miles from Middleton. She was looking forward to having a chance to talk to Molly about Evan, try to sort things out.

Gayle was also going home for the holiday. Before she left, she told Joy she was going to try to find out something that might give them a clue to what connection there might be between their two families, something that might help them sort out some of the coincidences.

Molly, plump, with rosy cheeks, silver curls, and merry bright eyes, greeted Joy happily. "Oh, darling, I'm so glad you're here. We have so much to catch up on. I can't wait for one of our old heart-to-hearts."

Molly's small bungalow was full of company. Molly held a constant open house. Her hospitality was famous, and there was a continual flow of friends in and out during the three-day holiday.

Her ladies' group met to pack baskets of food to distribute to needy families on their list. Then there was all the food preparation and cooking to be done for the dinner party, to which Molly always invited a dozen and welcomed any extras who came along.

On Thanksgiving Day they attended service at Molly's church and afterward went to the festive coffee hour.

A couple of times during her visit Joy started to bring up the subject of Evan, but every time either the phone rang or someone dropped by. It wasn't until the night before she had to return to the city that she at last was able to discuss Evan with Molly. Joy had intended to lead up to it, but after all the interruptions of the weekend, she just blurted it out.

"Is it serious, Joy?" Molly asked.

"That's what I don't know. I admire him tremendously, I enjoy being with him, we talk about everything—"

"And has he told you how he feels?"

"He's a man of few words, but I think I can tell . . ."

Molly sighed. "What can I say, Joy? Only you know what's in your heart."

"Why have you never married, Molly? I'm sure it's not for lack of opportunity. I've seen pictures of you when you were young. You were so pretty."

Molly smiled and touched her flyaway snowy hair and patted her double chin playfully. "That was then, this is now," she said with a laugh. "Well, Joy, my next question to you would be, how does Evan feel about your art career? You see, one reason I never married was because I don't believe you can have it all. I know, I know—people say you can, but I truly doubt it. At least in my day it was nearly impossible for a woman to have both a career—especially something as all-consuming as art—and a family. Nowadays some think you can. But at what cost? And to whom? What goes? Family life? What is neglected? Husband? Children? Art is a demanding priority. It was for me and others I knew who were serious about it. Artists have to be selfish to succeed."

Joy reflected that Molly was about the most unselfish person she knew. Hadn't she taken in an orphan teenager and given her a home, love, devotion? Molly seemed to have a rich, full life with her artwork, her friends, her activities. Still, Joy thought she understood what Molly was saying. Sometimes you have to make a choice. And that is not easy.

On the Monday after Thanksgiving, Joy was back at work. There were only two more panels to finish. The most dramatic one of all, she felt, would be the one with the centurion coming to Christ. She had still not approached Evan about posing. She was convinced that he would be perfect to represent the Roman officer. Everything about Evan made him a prime candidate—he could have been cast for the part in some Hollywood biblical spectacular.

Yet she felt shy about asking him. By his own admission, Evan's approach to life was scientific. It did not include faith. It precluded miracles. How would he feel being asked to be involved in this tremendous depiction of a miracle? Would he be angry, resent her placing him in the awkward position of having to refuse? She didn't know. Nevertheless, it kept nagging at her that she would never find out unless she asked. She would have to wait for the right time—and trust she would know when that was.

All this was on her mind as she painted. Suddenly she heard Evan's voice speaking to someone at the nurses' station. Calmly she mixed some cobalt blue to fill in the stripe at the edge of the paralytic's garment. Joy was trying to be as authentic as possible in costuming her figures. She had read in the Old Testament, in Numbers 15:38–40, that the Lord told the Jews to put a blue thread on the borders of their clothes so that when they saw the blue, they would remember God's holy purpose for their lives. Joy had been taught that God had a plan for everyone's life. What was the purpose of her life? God had given her the talent to paint. She wanted to be true to that calling, not allow anything to deter her from fulfilling it.

Her brush was poised when Evan came into the solarium. "Still here?" he demanded. "You keep long hours."

Joy swiveled to see him approach. "Look who's talking. So do you." She stood up stiffly, paintbrush still in hand, noticing that he looked tired. She suddenly realized what it must be like for Evan, what a toll it must take on him, dealing with life-and-death situations every day. Maybe today he had had to give a patient or his family a negative prognosis.

"Let's go somewhere, have something to eat, listen to some music," he suggested.

"Oh, I don't know. We've both had a long day. I'm afraid I wouldn't be very good company."

"You're always good company. Come on, don't say no. I need to go somewhere tonight where there's light, life, activity. I don't want to go alone. We'll eat and I'll take you right home, I promise."

"Evan, you're always feeding me!" she protested.

"We can't have any starving artists around here. Bad for the image of the hospital."

Joy laughed helplessly. "Okay."

She quickly cleaned up her brushes and put everything away, and they left the hospital together.

When they had seated themselves in Evan's car, he asked, "How was your holiday?"

"Very nice, very traditional," she replied. "Molly loves it that way. Dinner was fabulous. She cooks the turkey and makes the pies, and all the guests bring their prize dishes."

"What did you take?" He seemed genuinely interested.

"Well, mainly I fixed the centerpiece—fruit and flowers spilling out of a cornucopia basket . . ."

"Naturally, the artistic touch."

"Well, each person does what he or she does best."

"Fair enough."

"It was a busy, happy time. Molly's house is always filled with friends."

"Molly sounds like someone I'd like."

"I'm sure you would," Joy said. She almost added, "Someday you'll have to go down there with me and meet her," but she stopped herself, remembering Molly's warning about her involvement with Evan.

Slowing at a sign that read, "World's Best Pizza," Evan asked, "Pizza all right?"

"Sure."

As they pushed through the door, the sound of loud music engulfed them, along with the warm smell of garlic and tomato sauce. The place was crowded—mostly with the young crowd from the nearby college, since it was Friday night and a popular gathering place for students. Evan and Joy saw an empty booth in the back and headed toward it. As Joy slid in on the red plastic seat, she laughingly asked Evan, "Is this what you needed?"

He made a grimace. "Not exactly what I had in mind, but close. Anyway, I know they make a good pizza."

They ordered a large California combo to share. While they waited, they sipped on steaming coffee in thick white mugs. The music and voices and laughter all around made conversation nearly impossible. Evan shrugged and they smiled at each other. They were both tired anyway, so they simply absorbed the atmosphere surrounding them.

A few minutes later a boisterous group of young men came in and found a table that had just been cleared. When they started to sit down, two of them looked over at Joy and waved, calling, "Hi!" She smiled and waved back.

Evan glanced at the group, who were busy joking with the waitress amid much laughter. Then he gave Joy a questioning look.

"A couple of the guys I knew at college," she explained.

Pretty soon their pizza was served, and they both ate hungrily.

Later as Evan drove her home, Joy noticed that he was unusually quiet. At first she thought it was due to his fatigue, but she soon found out that wasn't it at all.

When he took her up the winding steps to her door, she asked, "Is something wrong, Evan? You haven't said a word since we left the pizza parlor."

"I was just thinking that maybe you'd rather be out with people your own age than with someone like me. Like those guys you knew from school—"

"Oh, Evan, they're just casual acquaintances. They were in one of my classes; I saw them on campus. I never went out with any of them." Joy felt awkward having to explain this, but it seemed important to Evan.

"I'm a lot older than you," Evan said.

"Evan, I never gave that a thought. It doesn't matter. I enjoy being with you, unless—" She paused.

"Unless what?"

"Unless you think I'm too young for you?"

His expression made her dissolve into laughter.

"Not in the least," he said. "I just wanted to be sure I wasn't—" Evan hesitated. "I really missed you while you were gone, Joy. How much even surprised me. Every time I passed the solarium, I found myself looking in, expecting to see you, and when I realized you weren't there—that you were a hundred miles away—it was then . . ." His voice trailed off. "Joy, I can't tell you what getting to know you has meant to me," he said quietly. "For a long time I've been unhappy, restless. Nothing I did or had or tried seemed to satisfy me. Until lately. Since I've met you and we've spent time together, that emptiness I used to feel is somehow gone."

Not knowing exactly what to say, Joy murmured, "If that's true, I'm glad."

"I hope I haven't made you uncomfortable by telling you this. I didn't mean to do that. I just wanted you to know."

Joy was silent.

"I'm glad you're back," he said softly. He put his hand on her chin, raised her face, and kissed her lightly, then turned and went quickly down the steps.

chapter
13

AT NOON ON MONDAY, Joy was seated at a table at the small Mexican restaurant where she and Gayle occasionally had lunch. It was their favorite place to eat, since it was near the hospital and both of them enjoyed the good food and quiet atmosphere.

That morning Gayle had caught Joy at the elevator as she was waiting to go up. "Can you meet me for lunch?" she had asked. "I have something to show you."

Gayle's unusually excited expression had made Joy curious, and she suggested the Adobe.

Now, watching Gayle as she arrived, Joy thought again that with her looks and regal carriage, Gayle could have been a high-fashion model.

As soon as they had ordered tacos, Gayle reached into her large shoulder bag and brought out a small, square, Zip-locked bag and handed it to Joy. It was a sepia daguerreotype of a black woman in a turban and a ruffled apron, holding in her lap a fair-haired little white boy about two years old.

"Who is this?" asked Joy.

"Look on the back."

Joy turned it over. Printed in block letters were the words "Baby Jonathan and me. Miss Rose give to me in 1860. Montclair Plantation, Mayfield, Virginia."

"How did you get this?"

"It belonged to my Great-Great-Grandmother Tilda. My mother showed it to me this weekend when I was home. I told her about you and how we met, about what you were doing at Good Sam's, and about the painting and your grandfather and all. Mom said Grandma Tilda always had this picture displayed in her house. She was an old woman when my mother was a little girl, but evidently she had been the nurse to this little boy. She must have loved him and his mother very much to cherish this picture all these years."

"Montclair, Mayfield, Virginia," Joy repeated.

The two stared at each other for a long time. Then Gayle said, "I know from the black history course I took in college that after emancipation, many freed slaves took the last names of their former masters, since slaves had been given only first names. That must be what happened to Tilda and her family. They came north from Virginia after the Civil War and took the name Montrose."

Joy held the picture, looking at it for a long time. It was like looking into the past, into another world, another time. Then she looked at Gayle. "You realize, don't you, Gayle, that we have a common background? All those years ago. Isn't it wonderful and meaningful that our paths happened to cross at Good Samaritan and we became friends?"

Later when Joy went back to her painting, her mind was totally preoccupied with thoughts brought by the image of that old picture. Who was Miss Rose, the woman who gave it to Gayle's great-great-grandmother? Who was baby Jonathan? And what about Tilda herself, who as a young woman seemed to have been so important in the lives of these people? How did it all relate to her own family history, to the father she had never known, Lt. (jg) Beaumont Montrose?

Joy determined that the next time she went to Molly's, she

would ask her what she knew about the Montrose family, into which Molly's cousin Anne had married.

Evan's voice broke into her thoughts. "Want to take a break, join me for coffee?"

She looked up at him. "No, thanks, I can't. I need to keep working."

He looked disappointed so she rushed on. "There is something I'd like to ask you, though."

"Ask."

"Would you do something for me?"

"Sure. You want me to bring you back a cup from the cafeteria?"

"No, it's . . .well . . ." All at once Joy decided now was the time to ask. "Would you pose for me?"

He looked startled. "Pose?"

"Yes, for one of the panels."

"You mean for the *mural,* the healing miracles mural? You've got to be kidding."

"No. I'm serious. I've thought about it a lot, and you'd be a perfect centurion."

"A what?"

"A Roman army officer. They called them centurions. They were occupying Israel at the time of Jesus. The Jews were a conquered people."

Evan's expression was one of both bewilderment and discomfort.

Joy hastened to offset his protest. "Oh, Evan, don't say no. I've looked and looked, and I've come to the conclusion that you are definitely the right person."

He raised one eyebrow quizzically. "What would I have to wear, some sort of toga or—"

"Oh no, nothing like that. All you'd have to do is pose. I could paint on the appropriate costume later. And anyway, it would be

107

more a plumed helmet sort of thing." She began to laugh at his doubtful grimace. "It will be practically painless, I promise."

"But what does this fellow have to do with the miracles? Did he have some kind of illness, or was he wounded in battle?"

"Evan, you mean you don't ... you've never heard about—" She stopped short. It seemed incredible to her that Evan was unfamiliar with this well-known incident in the Bible. However, she knew that the worst thing to do would be to embarrass him, so she said tactfully, "Wait a minute. I'll read the account of this. It's very short." She got up from her stool and dug into her tote bag for the pocket-size paperback edition of the New Testament she always carried with her.

"It's in the account written by Matthew, one of Jesus' disciples and an eyewitness to the miracles. Here's what he wrote about the centurion. Chapter 8, starting at verse 5."

As Joy read, Evan listened attentively.

> When Jesus had entered Capernaum, a centurion came to him, asking for help. "Lord," he said, "my servant lies at home paralyzed and in terrible suffering."
>
> Jesus said to him, "I will go and heal him."
>
> The centurion replied, "Lord, I do not deserve to have you come under my roof. But just say the word, and my servant will be healed. For I myself am a man under authority, with soldiers under me. I tell this one, 'Go,' and he goes; and that one, 'Come,' and he comes. I say to my servant, 'Do this,' and he does it."
>
> When Jesus heard this, he was astonished and said to those following him, "I tell you the truth, I have not found anyone in Israel with such great faith. . . ."
>
> Then Jesus said to the centurion, "Go! It will be done just as you believed it would." And his servant was healed at that very hour.

Joy finished reading and looked at Evan for his answer.

From his expression she could not tell what he was thinking, what he might say. He remained quiet, as though he were considering the matter. Then he smiled. "All right, for you I'll do it. I'll be your centurion. I may live to regret it, but I'll do it."

Evan did not want to pose at the hospital, despite Joy's assurance that once she added the centurion costume, no one would recognize the finished figure. She simply wanted to paint Evan's profile under the plumed helmet. However, to satisfy him they scheduled his modeling sessions for weekends at her place.

He was an impatient, restless model.

"You're worse than a child," Joy told him with pretended annoyance one day. "Debbie was a dream compared to you!" She threw down her pencil and closed her sketchbook.

"I thought you told me you read to her while she was posing. I don't get that treatment," Evan accused.

"Wrong. She read to me," Joy retorted.

"Well, where's the book? I'll read to you and see if it goes any better."

"The Velveteen Rabbit?" Joy scoffed.

"You said it has a powerful message for adults."

"So it has. Maybe that would be a good idea."

"Next time. We're going to dinner now," he announced.

Evan always insisted on taking her somewhere after the hour-long session was over. As the weeks went by, Joy realized they were spending more and more time together. They did things like going to a cinema that featured foreign films and classic movies, browsing in secondhand bookstores and record shops, patronizing an ice cream parlor, or sometimes just walking in the park. Simple things. Just the kind of things that lovers did together. With a shock Joy realized that was exactly what Ginny Stratton had accused her of doing.

Was she falling in love? Were *they* falling in love?

chapter

14

BY THE SECOND WEEK in December, the atmosphere at the hospital began to change. Christmas trees were set up on each floor, the nurses' stations were decorated, and Christmas music floated through the halls constantly. A subtle undercurrent of anticipation was tangible among the staff as they went about their duties. Nurses, orderlies, and LVNs all wore, pinned on their uniforms, bright little Christmas corsages made by the medical auxiliary.

Babies born during December were sent home in scarlet stocking buntings and little caps made by the Pink Lady volunteers. The hospital's gift shop was busier than ever. Florists made twice as many deliveries, bearing bright red, pink, or white poinsettias for patients.

On December 23, Santa Claus visited the pediatrics wing, and the air rang with the happy sound of children's excited voices and laughter.

A Christmas party for the doctors, nurses, and staff of the fourth floor was planned for five o'clock on Christmas Eve. Joy had received one of the few invitations extended to those who were not regular hospital personnel. Things were too hectic for her to work on the panels that day, so she stayed home and trimmed her tiny tree, decorated her apartment, and wrapped presents. She had asked Molly to handwrite in calligraphy the poem "Hyacinths for the Soul" to give to Gayle. She had bought Evan a copy of *Medusa and the Snail*, a book of essays by Lewis Thomas, a doctor-author. She debated about another gift she had for him. It was a watercolor of the road through autumn woods leading up to his cabin. She had painted it from sketches she'd made that day. Was it too personal, a reminder of all they had talked about—his telling her about Susan, his saying how much she herself had come to mean to him? Joy wrapped it anyway, thinking she would decide later whether or not to give it to him.

At four o'clock she dressed for the party. She had bent her budget a little by buying a new dress she had seen in a window at Shelton's, even though her employee discount was no longer in effect. She soothed her conscience somewhat by assuring herself that the dress would stay in style for years. It was dark green velvet with an empire waist and long fitted sleeves. She swept her hair up in a French twist and slipped on jade earrings. The effect was dramatic—she was sure no one at the hospital had ever seen her look so sophisticated.

Some of the staff were already at the party when Joy arrived. The staff lounge had been transformed by festive decorations. A tall tree sparkling with ornaments and lights dominated the room, and underneath its branches were piles of gaily wrapped gifts, all of which cost ten dollars or less. Each gift was tagged with the gender of the recipient. A drawing had been held to determine which type of gift to buy, and Joy's slip of paper had read, "Male." Her gift was a silk tie on which she had hand-painted a design. Secretly she hoped Evan would get it, but if not, she planned to paint another one especially for him.

She looked around for Gayle, Ginny, Aris, or Evan, but apparently none of them had come yet. She placed her present under the tree among the many others to be given out when Santa made his appearance.

Spotting Sister Mary Hope, Joy headed her way. They had hardly started to chat when Evan entered the room.

Joy's heart gave an unexpected leap when she saw him. Its pounding was so loud and fast, she wondered that with all the doctors in the room, one of them didn't rush to treat her for cardiac arrest.

Then Evan's sweeping glance around the room caught her, and he smiled and strode toward her. His eyes took her in, and he said in a low voice, "You look sensational. As soon as we can leave, I want to take you somewhere and show you off."

"But I'm leaving after this, Evan. I'm catching the nine o'clock bus down to Molly's. Have you forgotten? I'm spending Christmas with her."

He consulted his wristwatch. "That's four hours from now. There'll be plenty of time for us to eat dinner, and then I'll drive you to the bus station. All right?"

She felt too happy to say more than, "Fine."

"I guess I'd better mingle a little, destroy my reputation of being cold and aloof." He kept a straight face but his eyes were mischievous.

Joy pretended to be amazed. "I wouldn't say that."

"Wasn't that *your* first impression?"

"I think I was too dizzy to have any clear impression," she said, laughing as she remembered their collision that first day.

Evan laughed, too, then looked at her with tender amusement. Under the rising buzz of conversation in the room, he said in a low tone, "I'll make my social rounds, and then as soon as we can, we'll make our getaway."

The party crowd changed constantly as people came and left, going on or coming off various shifts of duty. Holiday greetings were exchanged against a background of Christmas music. Santa Claus made his appearance, and gifts were handed out amid much merriment. Things were still underway when Evan appeared again at Joy's side. He waited with some impatience for her to finish talking with one of the interns, then took her arm, saying, "I think it will be okay for us to leave now. I doubt if anyone will miss us."

They walked out from the hospital's overheated warmth into the cold, star-studded night and hurried to the physician's parking lot. As Evan got out his car keys, Joy was shivering, her teeth chattering a little.

"You're freezing!" he said. He grabbed her hands, then scolded, "You forgot your gloves." With that he slipped both her hands into the pockets of his fleece-lined jacket. Inside, one of Joy's fingers felt something small, square, wrapped in slick paper, tied with stiff ribbon.

Evan chuckled. "That's for you. A little Christmas present. Wait until we get in the car, and you can open it."

He opened the car door, helped her inside, then ran around and got in the driver's side. He turned on both the heater and the overhead light before handing her a tiny box wrapped in gold foil with a gilded bow.

She carefully tugged at the wrapping, and as the paper fell back, she saw that it was a small jewelry box. "Oh, Evan," she breathed. She almost said the cliché "You shouldn't have" but stopped just in time.

"Go ahead, open it."

"Evan, I hope—," she said hesitantly.

"Joy, just open it."

She lifted the box lid and saw nestled in the cotton a tiny honeybee pin, its body fashioned in alternate stripes of citrine and black enamel, its wings made of seed pearls.

"Like it?" Evan's voice was boyishly hopeful.

"Like it? I love it. It's exquisite, but—" She halted, and there was anxiety in her voice when she continued. "I'm not sure I should accept it."

"Why not, for Pete's sake?"

"Well, it must have been very expensive, and—"

"I can afford it," he said indulgently.

"It's not that. I mean, I'm not sure it's appropriate."

"Appropriate? Come on, Joy, you must be kidding. What would you consider an appropriate gift? A gift certificate to an art supply store?"

She had to laugh at the incredulous tone in his voice. "Why, Evan, how did you guess?"

"Look, it wasn't all that expensive. Anyway, I couldn't resist it. The minute I saw it in the jeweler's display window, it had your name on it. I had to get it for you. It's more than a Christmas present, Joy. It's a symbol of your faith," he said, then added, "which I envy."

"It's not to be envied, Evan," she said quietly. "It's available to everyone."

Evan didn't reply. He leaned forward and turned on the ignition. "Please, just wear it and enjoy it."

"Thank you, Evan," Joy said and pinned it on her lapel.

After stopping at Joy's car to grab her suitcase, her Christmas gift for Molly, and her canvas tote bag, they drove to the Edelweiss, a darkly paneled restaurant which had an alcoved fireplace and an intimate atmosphere and which specialized in Swiss food. On this holiday eve it was nearly deserted. Evan had ordered ahead and they were served promptly. The meal was simple but delicious, a cheese fondue and for dessert an apple strudel.

While they were having coffee, Joy said shyly, "I have something for you, Evan." From her tote bag she drew out the package she had wrapped for him in paper she had designed herself and placed it on the table. He looked at her, amused at her demeanor.

"Shall I wait until Christmas or open it now?"

115

"Now, so I can see if you like it."

"No question about that—I'm sure I will," he said. He unwrapped the small painting. "Oh, Joy, this is lovely. Something to always remember that day. Not that I'd ever forget it. Thank you."

Happy that he seemed pleased, Joy was glad she'd decided to give it to him. The waiter came to refill their cups, but Joy reluctantly checked her watch and said, "I guess we'd better leave. I can't miss my bus. It's the last one scheduled out tonight, and Molly's expecting me."

"Speaking selfishly, I wish you weren't going. I'm going to miss you. Terribly," Evan said with a rueful smile.

Joy didn't answer. She realized she would miss Evan, too. How much she wasn't sure.

They were quiet on the drive to the bus station, each bound in their own thoughts. Evan found a parking place and they hurried into the terminal.

The station bustled with the activity of holiday travelers. The loading platform was crowded with an assortment of passengers. The mood was jovial as they lined up to board, loaded with bundles, packages, shopping bags jammed full of brightly wrapped Christmas presents. The two of them stood with the rest of the crowd, Evan holding Joy's luggage. Finding conversation impossible, they just smiled at each other.

The bus driver finally ambled out, urged to hurry by the good-natured grumbling of the waiting passengers. He began to take tickets, drawling, "All right, folks, all aboard for the Jingle Bell Express." There was a ripple of appreciative laughter.

It was time to say good-bye, and strangely Joy felt a sudden reluctance to leave.

"Well, have a good holiday," Evan said, handing her the suitcase, the package, and the tote bag.

"You too, Evan, and thank you again for the pin. I love it."

116

"Good, I'm glad." His eyes lingered on her. "Don't forget we have a date for New Year's Eve."

"I won't."

"Let me know the minute you get back, okay?"

"Okay."

"You comin', lady?" the bus driver asked.

"I'd better go," Joy said.

"Merry Christmas, Joy," Evan said, putting both hands on her shoulders. Then he leaned down and kissed her.

"Merry Christmas, Evan," she replied, then quickly turned and hurried to where the driver was holding the bus door open for her.

"See you next week!" Evan called.

Inside, Joy pressed her face against the frosty window by her seat and saw that Evan was still standing on the platform, waving as the bus lumbered out of the station. He looked touchingly lonely. Her heart gave a tug. Somehow she longed to comfort him. But then the bus turned a corner and Evan was lost to sight. She leaned back against the seat, and an unexpected thought passed through her mind: *There'll be other Christmases.* Surprised, she straightened up. What did that mean? What was happening to her? Was she truly falling in love with Evan Wallace?

On Christmas Day, Molly's home, all decorated for the season, was alive with holiday festivities. Delicious smells permeated every corner of the cozy little house, and there was a constant stream of visitors who came bearing gifts and left with gifts from Molly.

It wasn't until the day after Christmas that Joy and Molly had a quiet time together to really talk. Molly nodded and made no comment as Joy expressed some of her thoughts and feelings about Evan. "He is so much different than I thought at first, Molly. So much gentler, more sensitive, and somehow vulnerable."

"Are you falling in love with him, Joy?"

"I've never really been in love, so I'm not sure. I enjoy being with him. I'm amazingly comfortable. Which is strange, because it's something I would never have dreamed would happen after my first impression of him."

"How does he feel about you?"

"I don't know." She showed Molly the honeybee pin. "I think he is interested, intrigued maybe. He doesn't share my faith but is sort of in awe about it."

Molly seemed concerned and hesitated a moment before saying, "Well, dear, my only advice for you is to pray." She paused again, then said, "I hope this won't interfere with your trip this summer? You still plan to go to France, don't you?"

"Oh yes, Molly. You know how long that's been my dream."

"Dreams sometimes have a way of being replaced by something you hadn't dreamed about."

"I'm not sure I understand your meaning."

"Often, in the guise of love, we sacrifice our own dreams to fulfill someone else's. Just be careful that doesn't happen to you, Joy."

Joy considered Molly's advice often during the next few days. She knew it was given in love, as always. In telling Molly about Evan, had she overemphasized his importance in her life?

All that week she kept thinking about him, wondering what he was doing, if he was lonely.

One evening after supper she had a chance to tell Molly about Gayle and the strange coincidences they had discovered. "Did my mother tell you much about my father's family?" she asked as they sat in the living room near the warmly lit fireplace.

"Not really," said Molly. "They were married such a short time. It was a whirlwind romance. As you know, she met him in San Diego when he was in flight training, and then he went overseas almost immediately and sadly was killed within a few months."

"I have a big void in my life, Molly, not knowing about my father. Especially since all this has come up. I have his name and nothing else."

"I have something perhaps you should have," Molly said. She got up and went over to her small desk and opened one of the drawers and took out a slim packet of envelopes. "Before your mother married Steve, she gave these to me. She said that when the time was right, she wanted her child to have them." She handed the small packet of envelopes to Joy. "These are letters your mother and father wrote to each other after Beau went overseas. They were both very young and very much in love."

Joy looked at the letters, then back at Molly.

"I think the time is right for you to read them, dear. Your mother felt she was starting a new life with Steve, and since you were so young, not quite three, she felt it would be better for you not to be confused. She wanted you, Steve, and herself to be a family. But she guessed that someday you might want to know about your real father."

Joy turned the letters over a couple of times. A strange sensation went all through her, as if she were about to open a door that had always been locked and walk through it. She had no idea what she would find on the other side, what message these letters would give her. She felt both excited and a little afraid.

"I'm going to bed now so you can be alone when you read them. They are very special and very private and will, I'm sure, be precious to you," Molly said, kissing her gently on her cheek. Then she left Joy sitting alone by the fire.

One by one Joy opened the letters and read them.

Dearest Beau,

You have only been gone a few hours, but I feel totally devastated. I don't know how I can bear this separation. I know you said it would only be a matter of months. I am trying to be brave, and I will be a good navy wife, I promise, and cope.

I love you always,
Anne

Precious Annie,

I wanted to tell you all this before I left, but somehow the words didn't come or come out right. I think you know how much I love you and will miss you. I miss you already and we've just said good-bye. In the short time I've known you (how many weeks has it been? Sometimes I feel I've known you forever. I know I will love you forever), you have made my life so complete. There was an emptiness in it that I didn't even know was there until you came and filled it.

I wish we had had time to go to Virginia so my mother and father could meet you, get to know and love you as I'm certain they would. I'm glad we opted for the small wedding on the base, with only the chaplain and Dick and Myrna to stand up for us. We had little enough time as it was, and since I'd just received my orders, I really was selfish enough to just want to have you to myself. I'll write again as soon as I can. Until then know that I consider myself the luckiest man in the world.

Ever yours,
Beau
Lt. (jg) Beaumont Montrose

Dearest Beau,

It still seems funny to me to get a letter addressed to Mrs. Beaumont Montrose. The first thing I do every evening when I get home from work is to check the mailbox see if there is a letter from you. I miss you so dreadfully.

Yours always,
Anne

There were several short, similar letters; then Joy came to another one:

Beau Darling,

The most wonderful news. I hope you will be as happy as I am to know we are going to have a baby. I know we talked about having a family someday, but it's going to be sooner than we thought. And I am so glad, because it takes away some of the loneliness to know that part of you is with me. Of course, I am sad that you won't be here with me to welcome him (or her?). But it won't be long now, will it? Your tour of duty will be over soon, and you'll be home with us— funny to say us!

Annie, My Love,

I've just been sitting here thinking of our future. It's going to be so great. I can't wait to take you and our baby back to Mayfield and show off both of you to my parents. I wrote Mom and Dad as much as I could about you, but meeting you in person is ten times better. I kept my promise and didn't tell them about the baby. That's your privilege. Mom said she had received a sweet note from you that included the pictures Dick took at our wedding. They are both anxious to meet you. They are going to Scotland this summer because my dad's mother has not been well and they want to visit her. That's something we'll do, too, sweetheart, when this whole thing is over and I'm back in the good old U.S.A. Did I tell you I have a bunch of relatives in Virginia that are all wanting to meet you and entertain us? You've never seen southern hospitality until you've experienced it Virginia-style. Our home, Montclair, has been in the family for generations, but it's not a fancy palatial mansion—just homey and welcoming. I think you'll love it. It's a great place for kids to grow up—there are horses, dogs, trees to climb, woods to play in. I can't wait to begin my life with you there, darling Anne. Take care and I'll write again soon.

That was the last letter in the pile. Joy looked at the date of the letter, then unfolded the yellowed telegram that was at the bottom. It was from the secretary of the navy.

We regret to inform you that your husband, Lt. (jg) Beaumont Montrose, died gallantly in action . . .

The date was only a few days after that of the last letter.

Tears rolled down Joy's face, and she didn't bother to wipe them away. She had looked into a piece of history, into two young lovers' hearts. Her mother had been nineteen, her father twenty-three. But they had left a living legacy of their love for their daughter.

Joy stayed an extra day because a friend of Molly's had planned a buffet dinner party especially to include her, so she did not get back to the city until late in the day of December 31.

Evan was at the bus station to meet Joy. He had called her at Molly's to find out what bus she was taking and when it would arrive.

When she got off the bus and saw him, Joy felt a surge of happiness. Slowly they moved toward each other. Evan was smiling as she had never seen him smile before. When he reached her, they stood for a moment, just looking at each other. He took her face in both hands, lifted it, and kissed her, then said, "Welcome back."

Their kiss seemed the most natural thing to have happened. When it ended, Joy's head felt a little dizzy, almost exactly as it had after their first encounter, when they bumped into each other outside the hospital elevator. Remembering that, Joy laughed a little.

"What's funny?" Evan asked, picking up her suitcase and tucking her hand through his arm as they walked to his car.

"I was just thinking about how we met."

"That was a long time ago. Months. It seems like light-years. I feel as if I've known you forever."

They walked through the frosty early evening air to the parking lot. He opened the car door for her and she got in. He came around the other side and settled in behind the wheel, then turned to her. The light from the dashboard illuminated her face, and he leaned over and kissed her again. "I missed you, Joy."

"I missed you, too, Evan," Joy said, realizing just how much she really had, how much having him there waiting on the bus station platform had meant to her. "I'm sorry if you made plans for New Year's Eve . . ."

"My only plan was spending it with you."

"Did you want to go somewhere?"

"Not really. Did you?"

"Actually, I'm pretty tired. It's been a busy week."

"Then I'll take you home."

On the way, Evan drove with one hand on the steering wheel, and with the other hand he reached for Joy's. "Did I tell you I missed you?"

"Yes, Evan, you did," she said, laughing.

"Did I tell you I was also going to feed you?"

"No, but that's your usual M.O."

"I had the Pampered Gourmet fix us a special dinner. All we have to do is pop it in your microwave and open the bottle of chilled sparkling cider. How does that sound?"

"You think of everything, don't you?"

"I try," he said, squeezing her hand before he released it and turned into the gate leading to Joy's water tower apartment.

They ate leisurely in Joy's intimate little dining area, sharing some of the events of the week they'd been apart. Evan supplied hospital news, while Joy described some of the homey details of her holiday.

"People are giving the mural rave reviews," Evan told her.

"Wait until they see the centurion panel," she teased.

"One thing has become very clear to me this week," Evan said, making a toasting gesture with his glass. "I've fallen in love with you, Joy."

Instinctively Joy drew back. "Oh, Evan, I never meant that to happen."

"Oh, my darling, you're such a child. Couldn't you see this was happening?" Evan said very gently. "How in the world could I resist you?"

All the warning flares went up, but Joy was too dazzled to see them. Evan leaned across the table, searching her face, then kissed her with great sweetness.

Before she could react, they heard the sound of whistles blowing, factory horns blaring, church bells ringing out through the wintry night.

Evan stood up, held out his hand, drew her up onto her feet, and with his arm around her waist led her out onto the small balcony outside her door. There he took her slowly into his arms. "Happy New Year, sweetheart," he said and kissed her.

An hour later Evan was gone. The apartment seemed cold, empty, and full of shadows. Joy stood at the window looking out. More snow had fallen, drifting over the benches and gathering on the lampposts of the park across the way. A misty moon shone through the dark, bare branches of the trees, which resembled etchings on white paper.

The windowpane was frosted, and she pressed her face against it and with her finger drew two hearts on the icy glass, scratched "JM" and "EW" in the centers.

He loves me and he knows I love him. At first Joy felt that her heart might burst with the wonder of it. It was like skyrockets going off within her. But then, like skyrockets that light up the sky for a few seconds before fizzling out and dropping into darkness, her feeling of elation fell away, leaving her somber and shaken.

If this love was real, what was she to do about it? Up until now her dreams, her hopes, her plans had all been for herself. All her life, love had been in short supply, yet she had managed to live without it. She had never dreamed that love would come to her like this, that a man like Evan would fall in love with her.

In spite of the things Evan had pointed out which they had in common, such as the fact that they were both alone in the world, without close relatives or family (Evan's parents had died when he was in medical school, his only brother in a car accident years ago), their lives were still worlds apart. He was a successful surgeon, she a struggling artist. Could their love bridge these differences?

Joy did not know. She would have to decide. But first, as Molly had advised, she would have to pray about it.

chapter

15

BACK AT THE HOSPITAL Joy was anxious to tell Gayle about what she had found out about her parents during the holidays. The fact that her father was from Mayfield, Virginia, and lived in a place called Montclair seemed another strange coincidence linking the two young women.

She showed Gayle the last letter Beau Montrose had written to his young wife, describing his home. After Gayle read it, she looked at Joy. "Then it must be as I thought. My ancestors were slaves of the Montrose family and lived at Montclair."

"Isn't it incredible that neither of us knew anything about this and both ended up here at Good Samaritan?"

This common thread made their friendship closer. Gayle and Joy began to see each other at least once or twice a week. It wasn't just that they shared a historical background but that they genuinely liked each other and enjoyed being together.

The lovely white snow of January merged into the grimy slush of February, in which new storms dusted a fresh layer over still-unmelted piles along ice-slick roads. People lost hope of ever seeing bare ground again. To make matters worse, torrential rain then turned the dirty snow into a kind of mire.

Joy usually was unaffected by weather, but now the unrelenting gray days seemed depressing. She began waking with an uncharacteristic heaviness of heart. She was plagued by doubts about her involvement with Evan. Besides this or maybe because of it, she was experiencing a block in her painting. The work that had brought her so much satisfaction now left her unfulfilled at the end of the day. She returned home drained with the effort. She had trouble sleeping and would wake up during the night, troubled about her relationship with Evan and worried about finishing the panels.

Three of them were completed, and everyone had praised her finished work. Of the two that remained to be done, the one that was causing her the most difficulty was the painting of the centurion. None of the sketches she had made of Evan were satisfactory. A reluctant model, after a few minutes he would demand, "Isn't that enough? I need to stretch."

The fact that he was self-conscious about posing was not the main problem. After all, Joy had sketched children who wiggled and moved with almost every breath. In her life classes at art school, they had worked with every sort of model, and she was good at getting quick likenesses. No, she concluded, the real problem was her own confused feelings about Evan.

Joy suspected that the hospital grapevine buzzed about the two of them. Nobody could have missed seeing them together in the cafeteria or leaving together, heading for Evan's car. At the hospital, one person's whisper became wild rumors.

Remembering Molly's tactful questions about how her relationship with Evan might damage her own plans for the future, Joy knew she would have to make a decision before they got more deeply involved. She remembered again Molly's advice to pray about it.

Joy procrastinated, almost knowing what the answer might be. However, trying another of Molly's suggestions, she began to search her Bible. To her dismay she seemed to turn repeatedly to 2 Corinthians 6:14–15: "Do not be yoked together with unbelievers. . . . What does a believer have in common with an unbeliever?" She knew Evan did not share her faith. He tolerated her faith, perhaps even envied her a little for it; however, he really didn't seem to think it was important. But it was. More important than even Joy had realized when she first went looking for life's answers. Her faith had sustained her through many of the traumas of her early life—losing her mother, being without a real home, finding her own way in the world. Without that bedrock faith, none of the things she had accomplished would have been possible. The mural, for example. Especially the mural.

After one of these forays into Scripture, Joy would shut the Bible, knowing she was trying to find some support for her emotions, not real guidance. Giving up her relationship with Evan would not be easy. But more and more a part of her knew she had to do it. When and how she would tell him, she wasn't sure.

While in this state of indecision, Joy found it harder and harder to go to the hospital each day to work on the mural. She also tried to avoid Evan. His presence was disturbing—it blurred her own clear-cut vision of her future. But how could she tell Evan? So she kept putting it off simply by juggling her routine. She started coming to the hospital at odd hours, during his office hours or at times when she knew Evan would be in surgery. Some days she found she could not work at all. She would make the attempt to start, then find she was too distracted, too tense, too conscious of the possibility that Evan would show up while she was still undecided about what to say or do.

One day she did not make her escape soon enough. Knowing he would be in surgery, she went in late. She had been working for about an hour when he suddenly appeared. He gave her a long, hard look, then said, "If I were the suspicious sort, I might think you'd been dodging me all week."

Caught unprepared, Joy tightened the cap on the tube of ochre she was holding and replaced it in her paint box without answering.

"Well, am I wrong? Or have you been avoiding me?"

"Not exactly."

"What does that mean, 'Not exactly'?"

When she didn't reply, Evan went on. "I've come in here at different times all week looking for you." He paused. Joy felt the rush of embarrassment warm her face. "It doesn't look as if you've made much progress on the mural, either," he continued. "Is there something wrong? Something I don't know about? I check almost every day."

Joy's throat constricted painfully. "Evan, we need to talk."

"Good. Let's go for coffee."

Once they were seated in the booth with their coffee, he demanded, "So what's this all about?"

Joy had meant to lead up to it, but now she just blurted out, "I've come to a decision, Evan. I didn't mean for us to get this involved—I don't think we should see each other any more."

He looked shocked, then grim. "Why not?"

"Well, it's just that . . . your position and all, and my being here, people seeing us together. It just starts a lot of talk, and I don't think . . ."

"Ah, *that's* it! Afraid we'll end up on the pages of one of those tabloids at the checkout counter?"

"Well, of course not. But I don't like people talking about me."

"Look, Joy, I've been around hospitals long enough to know that people will talk about anything they can find to talk about. It doesn't mean anything. Soon something juicier comes along that they can discuss. A hospital grapevine is faster than any computer. Gossip is the fuel that runs the place—the hotter the item, the faster it travels."

"Evan, I'm serious," she started again.

"Okay, but I don't think this is the time or place to discuss it. I have to be in a meeting in ten minutes. It can wait. Will you have dinner with me tonight?"

She began to shake her head.

He frowned. "I have surgery in the morning, so it will be an early evening. I'll meet you at five, and we'll go from here."

Not waiting for her to refuse, Evan got up and with only a curt nod left the cafeteria, leaving Joy upset. She had not handled it well, not in the tactful, gentle way she had meant to— but when Evan was in a forceful, take-charge mode, there was no use trying to talk to him.

She rehearsed how she could explain it best without hurting him. She would just say that there wasn't room for romance in her life right now, that she had long-held plans to go abroad, to study art . . . Joy sighed. Tonight she would try to do a better job of explaining.

With all her good intentions, when Joy attempted to bring up the subject that evening at dinner, Evan cut her off. "I don't want to hear this, Joy. Don't you understand that I love you? I want us to get married."

Joy gasped. He had never mentioned marriage before.

"I know this isn't the romantic way you would like it, nor even how I wanted to say it," Evan continued briskly. "But surely you must have realized that my feelings for you go deeper than friendship?"

She shook her head. "Evan, I can't marry you. I don't plan to marry at all—at least for a long time. I want to paint and—"

He didn't let her finish. "Of course. I know that, Joy. Getting married has nothing to do with that. You can go on painting."

"Not the way I intend to paint. You don't understand. To

me, painting is not a hobby, not a pastime. I want to be really good. That takes work. Maybe years of work. And dedication. It has to come first. It means study, and I have so much to learn. With the money I earn from the mural, I plan to go to Europe. I may decide to stay there, if I can get apprenticed to an artist I admire or take classes. I understand you can live cheaply in Italy or France, and—"

"But Joy, darling, I can take you to Europe, to France, Italy, wherever."

"No, Evan. I have to do this on my own."

He looked at her for a long time, and she could not help but be aware of the tenderness in his gaze.

Finally he said, "Whether you think so or not, I do understand what you're saying. I admire you tremendously—your drive, your ambition. Why should marriage interfere with the fact that I want to help you, support you?"

Joy felt a rush of gratitude for the love shining from his eyes. It was a love that was hard to resist. Evan only wanted to make things easier for her, help her attain her goals, maybe even sooner than she could alone. She felt herself weakening. Yet almost immediately she felt the nudge of her conscience. *Unequally yoked*. Evan had said nothing about sharing her faith. That would always be an unresolved issue between them. Sooner or later she would have to make a clean break of the relationship. If she stayed in it . . . She thought of Ginny Stratton and her affair. She remembered Ginny's confiding, "I can't seem to find the strength to break it off." Joy had seen firsthand Ginny's struggle, how her relationship had robbed her of her values. Joy suppressed a shudder. It could happen to her too.

Evan glanced at his wristwatch. "We can't get into this tonight, Joy. I have early surgery tomorrow. All I can do is reassure you I would never do anything to interfere with your art career, what you want to do. I just want to be there to support you and help you reach your goals."

"Evan, I know that and I appreciate it, but it just wouldn't work—"

"Please, Joy, let's wait to discuss this. I have to go to a medical conference in New Orleans at the end of the week. I want you to take the time to think this through, consider marrying me. I'm not trying to rush you or pressure you. I do love you."

Resignedly Joy agreed that when Evan got back from New Orleans, they would have a long talk.

For the remainder of that week they only saw each other briefly at the hospital. It was a relief for Joy because she was still dealing with mixed emotions.

Evan Wallace was strong, caring, compassionate. What marriage to him could offer her was everything she had never known—security, devotion, financial freedom. It was all she had ever needed. But was it more than she wanted? She had worked hard to be independent, to build a career, to make it on her own. How could she be free if bound by love? All her thinking only made her more confused, more uncertain.

At those times she would leave the fourth floor and take the elevator to the ground-floor chapel. There she would slip into one of the pews and pray for guidance and the strength to follow it.

Was she being selfish to want to fulfill her own dreams? She truly believed God had placed in her heart this deep desire to be an artist. If she were to pursue it, weren't marriage and a family out of the question, at least for years? Joy knew that Evan would not be willing to wait for years.

One morning as Joy was waiting for the elevator to take her up to fourth, she was surprised when the door opened and Ginny Stratton stepped off.

"Going off duty. I changed my shift," Ginny explained. "I'm working nights now."

Taken aback, Joy asked, "Do you like it better?"

Ginny made a comic face. "Well, I asked for it. It keeps me off the streets and out of singles bars," she said flippantly. "Actually, it was self-preservation. Survival. Want to join me in the cafeteria, and I'll tell you about it?"

Over coffee Ginny said, "I've stopped seeing Cliff." Her tone was matter-of-fact but there was an edge to it. "To tell you the truth, *you* are more or less responsible for my doing it. Oh yes, you are. Or those panels. Maybe a combination of both. Mostly my own guilt about the relationship. Or as we used to say in the church I grew up in, 'conviction of sin.' I don't use fancy words anymore to describe what I was doing. 'Affair' sounds so glamorous. But there was nothing glamorous about what we had. Sleazy is more like it. I finally woke up. I realized he was never going to divorce his wife. I was just a fling and there'd be others. Maybe there were even others while we were doing our thing." Ginny shrugged.

Joy could hear the pain in Ginny's voice under the bravado. "So how do you feel?"

"Rotten. Frankly, it's been rough. But I knew I had to do it. I've had help. I've started going to church again, and through some people there I've found a great support group. I'm beginning to see there's more to life than waiting for the phone to ring, arranging meetings, fitting into someone else's time schedule. . . . It'll be okay." Ginny stood up, put on her jacket over her uniform, gathered up her bag. "And I want you to know, you've been an inspiration, Joy, so thank you."

"Thank *me*? I had nothing to do with it. Jesus is the Healer," Joy said, hoping that didn't sound too sanctimonious.

Ginny smiled. "I know. Maybe you just reminded me."

Joy went home deep in thought. Had meeting Ginny just now been merely happenstance, or was it divine coincidence?

Opening the front door to her apartment that evening, Joy heard her phone ringing. It was Evan.

"How is New Orleans?" she asked.

"Lonely."

"Oh, Evan, come on. From what I've read, it's a fabulous town. Fantastic food, entertainment—"

"Wild rumors. It's a hotel room, a hamburger and milk via room service. Frustrating hours of trying to reach my girl by phone."

Joy gripped the receiver. He'd said, "my girl." Hadn't he absorbed anything she had tried to tell him?

There was a pause, one that evidently Evan noticed, because he quickly said, "Listen, Joy, I've been doing a great deal of thinking about us, and I want you to know I understand that you need your independence. But there's something else that's equally important, and I want you to give it some thought, okay?"

"And that is?"

"What we have found together is pretty rare in this crazy world—mutual trust, respect, honesty, friendship. And we should treat it carefully, not let it slip away by being afraid of what other people might say or suspect or imagine. We know who we are and what we're all about. I don't want to stop seeing you. I don't want to lose you."

"Evan, I—"

"Just promise you'll think about what I've said, and when I get back we'll talk about it. Promise?"

"I promise."

When Joy hung up, she hoped that agreeing to further discussion about their relationship hadn't given Evan false hope. Oh, why was everything so complicated?

It was easier to work on the panels without Evan's presence. Loving though it was, it kept her from completely concentrating on her work. She suspended work on the centurion panel even though she had finally achieved some fine sketches of Evan that were usable in the scene she envisioned. So far she had only chalked in the figure of the Roman soldier. Gradually she came to the conclusion that until she had come to some definite resolution about the future of her relationship with Evan, it would be impossible to complete.

The portrait of Evan she envisioned was strong. It became fixed in her mind as the barrier between her and her artistic career goal. If she allowed him to smooth the way for her, it would rob her of her own satisfaction of accomplishment. She needed to prove something, if only to herself.

Joy wasn't sure quite when it happened, but one morning she awoke with a new excitement, enthusiasm. Somewhere she had got a fresh insight into the unfinished panel of the centurion. She couldn't wait to get to the hospital and work on it.

Like the centurion, Evan was a man of power, prestige, authority. He gave an order and nurses, interns, residents scrambled to carry it out without question. He was known to be demanding but fair, a man of character.

The figure she had chalked in was in a standing position, in full military regalia, his helmet under one arm, the other arm flung out as though discoursing. Now that pose didn't seem right. Joy studied the panel, trying to imagine what was going through this proud Roman officer's mind and heart. How he must have battled his own pride, thinking what his fellow officers, his comrades—hardened warriors, veterans of many campaigns for Caesar—might say if they knew he went to a Jewish faith healer to seek help for a favorite servant. Even though it must have been a struggle for the centurion, his affection for this young man must have been great for him to overcome his pride, risk his reputation, humble himself.

He had put aside all of his pride and gone, and of him it was written that Jesus said, "I have not found anyone in Israel with such great faith."

Suddenly Joy understood the man's reason for doing it. He had come to an inner knowledge of who Jesus really was, that he was a man of greater power than his own. Someone who had command over life and death. A person to whom obeisance was due. Yes, that was it. The centurion would not have taken an arrogant, soldierly stance before Jesus. The posture was wrong.

She knew what the problem was. She opened her can of gesso, got out a wide-tipped brush, and began whiting out the figure as she had originally drawn it. That done, she went about setting up her palette and mixing the colors. With sure strokes she began to block in a new figure. This time it would be right. This time the centurion would be in a kneeling position.

Unaware of the passing hours, Joy painted, intently and with new confidence. She did not stop for lunch or anything else, and only when she noticed that the light had begun to fade did she glance at her watch and realize she had been working nonstop all day.

She sat back on her heels, surveying the panel with critical detachment. She knew she had painted an idealized version of the face, lending it an air of nobility and classic perfection. But the basic characteristics were Evan's. Joy realized she had painted the face of the man she loved.

Part 2

chapter
16

THAT EVENING AS Joy left the hospital and walked outside, heavy gray clouds hung in the darkening sky. There was a bitter chill in the air. The revelation she had had in front of the centurion mural weighed upon her heart. If she loved Evan, what should she do about it?

Her mind was in a turmoil as she drove home, stopped at her mailbox, and picked up her mail. Her steps were slow as she went up the stairway, her thoughts troubled. Inside she put down her mail without looking through it and went right to the kitchen, put on the teakettle.

She knew that when Evan returned from the medical conference in New Orleans, he would expect some kind of answer. She dreaded that moment. How could she hide the truth from him in spite of her words of denial? Wouldn't he see in her eyes the answer he wanted?

While the water was heating, Joy distractedly sifted through her mail. Among the sheaf of envelopes and advertisements was a long, white legal-size envelope. The return address immediately caught her attention: Lawrence and Bidewell, Attorneys at Law, Mayfield, Virginia. What on earth could this be? She tore it open and drew out the letter. Her eyes raced down the two pages so fast, she was merely skimming the sentences. Then she got to the last paragraph:

If you will provide us with a copy of your birth certificate, duly certified by a notary public and signed by two witnesses, proving that you are indeed Joy Montrose, daughter of Beaumont Montrose and Anne Layton, we will process the transfer of the property known as Montclair. Please contact us at the first possible date so this can be expedited.

The shrill whistle of the teakettle startled Joy. She grabbed a hot pad and poured the boiling water over her tea bag, still stunned at the contents of the letter. Her knees felt shaky, and she sat down on one of the kitchen stools and reread it.

With the death of Miss Heather Montrose and as the executors of her will, we are instructed to inform you that as the only remaining member of the family, and the direct descendant of Fraser Montrose, your grandfather, you have hereby become the heir and owner of the house and land known as Montclair.

No matter how many times Joy read the letter, she still couldn't believe it. After a while she called Molly and read it over the phone to her.

"Do you think it's some kind of joke?" she asked Molly.

"Hardly," was Molly's reply. "With all that legal language. The best thing to do is to call them and verify it, then send them what they asked for. It looks as though you've become a property owner, Joy."

Joy found it hard to sleep that night. She couldn't wait until the next morning to make the call to the lawyers and then tell Gayle. Montclair, which loomed so large in both their backgrounds, really did exist and was not just some myth or long-ago romantic tale.

The conversation with Mr. Lawrence, the attorney, lasted only about ten minutes, but it changed Joy's life forever.

"Since Miss Montrose never married and was getting on in years and had been in failing health, she had us searching for you quite a while ago. We didn't know if your stepfather had adopted you and if you were going by his name, so that delayed us. Unfortunately, Miss Montrose passed away before we located you. She did, however, write a letter that was to be given to you if our search was successful. I believe it contains instructions as to what she wanted done with stored family heirlooms, artifacts, paintings, and other memorabilia.

"Montclair was at one time famous for its thoroughbred horses. It was also a tobacco farm. The land of course has not been farmed productively for many years. Some of it was sold off by Miss Heather in the last few years for financial reasons. But the house and the twenty acres surrounding it are still quite valuable. I urge you to come down as soon as you can arrange it, to view the place yourself, make these decisions."

Joy hung up the phone, feeling very weak. She had inherited a mansion, valuable land, antiques, silver, the belongings of a wealthy family. She who had always struggled to make ends meet, worked hard just to keep up current expenses, now owned a plantation house in Virginia. It was unbelievable.

Her next call was to Gayle, who was just about to leave for the hospital.

"Can I catch you later?" Gayle asked. "I've got to make rounds."

"But this is important, Gayle. To both of us. Listen." Joy read the letter to her and told her about her conversation with the lawyer.

There followed a long pause, and then Gayle asked, "Well? Are you going?"

"I don't know. I haven't had time to think about it. I mean, it's too overwhelming. I never dreamed that anything like this would ever happen to me." Joy shook her head. "I never knew anything about my father's family—the Montrose family. Just what you and I have pieced together."

"I think you should go, Joy."

"Oh, Gayle, I feel so inadequate to deal with all this alone. I've had no experience in talking to lawyers or real estate people or—"

"Yes, but aren't you curious? This might provide the answers to all the questions you've always had about your family background. And he says there are things you've inherited that you're going to have to make decisions about. No one else can do that."

"I know," Joy sighed. Then she asked impulsively, "Would you go with me, Gayle? Montclair is your family home, too."

There was another long pause. "Well, in a slightly different way, of course."

"Yes, I know, but still . . . Oh, please, Gayle, come with me."

"Okay. Why not? If you can leave this morning, so can I. As it turns out, I'm already free tomorrow and Sunday, and I can arrange to take a couple more days off and make it a long weekend."

"How shall we go? By train or bus?" Joy thought for a moment. "But that would take forever. Plane? No, too expensive."

"I'll drive," Gayle said decisively. "We can take my car. Let's see. Mayfield is near Williamsburg, right? That's about 250 miles. The drive will take us about four or five hours. It will still be early when I finish my rounds, so if we leave right away, we should get there by this afternoon. That will give us enough time to go out to Montclair and look it over while it's still light."

"Oh, thank you, Gayle. I feel much better about it now that you're going with me."

"You know what I thought you had to tell me when you said it was very important?"

"No, what?"

"That you and Evan Wallace were engaged."

Joy gasped. "You did? What made you think that?"

"Well, it's pretty obvious how he feels about you."

"I hope you're the only one who thinks that," Joy said. ". . . You are, aren't you?"

There was a significant pause before Gayle answered. "You know hospitals."

Joy hesitated, then decided to confide in Gayle. "Truthfully, he *has* asked me to marry him, Gayle, but I've said no. I'm not ready to get married to anyone. You know my plans for the summer, as soon as the mural is finished. . . . Well, anyway, marriage isn't in those plans."

"He won't be easy to convince," Gayle said.

"I know. But he'll have to understand."

"I hope you're right. Breakups are so hard—they leave a residue of bitterness no matter what. Well now, about our trip . . . ," Gayle said, changing the subject to the details they would need to take care of before leaving.

Joy was relieved, not only that Gayle had agreed to go with her but that they would be gone when Evan returned from New Orleans. That way she could put off a little longer telling him her decision.

They were to meet at Good Samaritan as soon as Gayle made morning rounds. Joy quickly drove to the hospital and sought out Ginny. Ginny's eyes widened as Joy told her where she was going and why.

"Would you do me a favor, Ginny, and put this note in Evan's box in the doctor's lounge? He won't be back from the medical conference in New Orleans until after I'm gone." Joy handed Ginny her hastily written note explaining her journey.

"Okay, but he isn't going to like it," Ginny told her.

chapter

17

AT THE MAYFIELD sign they took the off-ramp from the expressway and headed for the center of town. Mr. Lawrence, the lawyer, had informed Joy that the keys to Montclair would be available at Tedroe Realty on Main Street.

Gayle found a parking space right in front of the office. Armed with the letter and her identification, Joy went inside.

The Realtor seemed surprised when she introduced herself. He hurriedly slipped on his suit coat, which had been draped on the back of his chair, and stood up. "Well, mighty nice to meet you. I'm Asa Tedroe." He extended his hand. "I didn't know you'd be here so soon. Mr. Lawrence just told me last week that he'd finally located Miss Montrose's kin."

Immediately he started rummaging in his desk drawer, pulling out key ring after key ring, examining the tags on each as he spoke. "Haven't been any Montroses around here in a good long time." He dropped the keys into a small brown-paper envelope, scrawled the name Montclair and some directions on it, and handed it to her. "Only Miss Heather living out at Montclair. In the last several years her health declined. She never was strong. Had polio as a child that weakened her considerably. Then after her younger brother Beau was killed"—he shook his head—"that near finished her. She was never the same after that. She adored him, you see. He was seventeen years younger. Almost more like her son than a sibling. She became a kind of recluse." He paused. "But she was sharp right to the last. Got all her affairs in order. That's how Mr. Lawrence was finally able to contact you." His eyes squinted a little, regarding her. "I reckon you'll be planning to sell the place? If so, I'd sure like to list it. We're the oldest realty firm in the county." He smiled. "Ask anyone hereabouts—they'll tell you that, Miss Montrose."

Not wanting to make any hasty commitment with so many things unresolved, Joy simply took the envelope and said, "Well, thank you, Mr. Tedroe. I'll have to talk to Mr. Lawrence, since he's handling the estate. I have an appointment with him tomorrow."

"Oh, by the way, Miss, in case you were going out there planning to stay, there's no electricity. Was turned off shortly after Miss Montrose's death."

Back in the car Joy told Gayle, "I've got the keys and the directions out to Montclair. We take the second left after the traffic light at the corner. That puts us on the old county road. We stay on that until we come to a stone wall. There are wrought-iron gates we pass through that lead up to the house." Joy spilled the contents of the envelope onto her lap, examining the key tabs. "One looks like a padlock key, so the gates might be locked. Then it's about a quarter mile up to the house."

They drove through town and took the turn onto a two-lane country road. A light rain began to fall, and Gayle switched on the windshield wipers. Their whisking sound was the only noise in the small car. Filled with a sense of anticipation mixed with excitement, neither of them spoke.

When they came in sight of a stone wall with tall iron gates, Gayle slowed the car. "That must be it."

Joy jumped out of the car and ran to the gate. There was a padlock on the gate handle. She hunted for the right key and inserted it into the rusty lock. After a few attempts she managed to turn it, loosening the metal padlock. Using both hands and all her strength, she pushed the gate open enough so Gayle could nose the small car through. When she got back into the car, Joy's face and hair were misted.

"Okay, here we go," Gayle said, shifting into low gear.

As they started up the narrow driveway, Joy was aware of strange sensation. The drive approaching the house suddenly seemed familiar, as if she had known it in some distant way all of her life. It was as if it were a place somehow lodged in the memory of her heart.

She glanced over at Gayle to see if she was having any of the same feelings. But Gayle was staring straight ahead, her capable hands on the wheel of the car, competently guiding it over the rutted, overgrown lane toward the house.

The mist added a luminosity to the scene. Joy leaned forward, peering through the crescent arc made by the windshield wipers. Through the silver gray veil of rain, the lacy froth of pink and white dogwood blossoms, she saw the blurred outline of the house appear. Montclair! It looked like something out of a dream.

Joy's breath became shallow. Strangely, she felt as if she were coming home to a place she had never been.

Gayle slowed the car to a stop. Nothing was said. Both young women seemed caught in some kind of spell.

After a few minutes, as if on silent cue, they both got out of the car and looked up at the house. At close range the effects of the time during which it had stood empty became obvious. It also looked as if over the years the house had been randomly enlarged, as if it had met the changing needs of the family who had lived there. Instead of spoiling it, this gave it a kind of charm. It appeared to be not an empty house of sad memories but rather one that still had a life of its own, a survivor bravely standing despite the ravages of time.

Once real people had lived here, Joy realized—her ancestors, the family from whom she'd come. Her own father, Beaumont Montrose, had grown up here, had left this house to go off to marriage and war, and had cherished the memory of his home, as he'd written in the letter to his bride shortly before he'd been killed.

It was getting dark. The sprinkle had turned into rain.

"Think you want to go inside?" Gayle asked.

"I don't know," Joy answered, fingering the keys.

"Since there are no lights, maybe we'd better find a motel and get a room for the night," Gayle suggested gently. "We can come back out early tomorrow."

"Yes, I guess that's the best idea," Joy agreed.

They returned to the car. Gayle backed up and turned around, then started down the drive. Joy looked back and caught a last glimpse of Montclair gleaming pale and lovely on the hill. She felt a kind of fierce pride. It was, after all, *her* heritage.

She sighed. What was to become of it? If she were to sell it, the buyer might subdivide the property and develop it. But how could she possibly keep it? On the other hand, how could she even think of letting it go?

On the way back to town, both Joy and Gayle were wrapped in a kind of melancholy. They had touched the past and it lingered hauntingly.

They found a Howard Johnson's motel, where they registered, then went to the coffee shop off the lobby. They ordered soup, hamburgers, and coffee, and Joy expressed some of her concerns.

"When I first learned I'd inherited it, it seemed like a windfall. Now that I've seen it, I don't know. It would need a great deal of restoration."

"The taxes alone on a place that size could bankrupt a person," Gayle suggested.

"Yes. The lawyer told me that the state already has liens against the property for back taxes that have begun to accumulate. Realistically, it may be more of a liability than an inheritance."

"Maybe you could arrange to give it to the state as a historic landmark?"

"That's a possibility. Virginia is very history conscious. A house like Montclair, which was built before the American Revolution and remained in the same family all this time, should be attractive to a heritage society." Joy took a sip of coffee, then sighed. "I should talk to the lawyer about it. There's so much to think about. . . ."

"And pray about," Gayle said quietly.

Saturday morning they decided that to make best use of their short time, they should move out to the house. Camp out, actually, but they had come prepared. They had both brought sleeping bags in case they couldn't find a motel on the trip. After a quick breakfast Gayle suggested they get a floor plan of the house, so they stopped at Tedroe's Realty again.

As he went to his file cabinet, the Realtor asked, "So how did you find the place, Miss Montrose? Not in too bad a condition, I hope? That is, other than some cobwebs and dust?"

Although he seemed inclined to conversation, Joy did not want to be delayed. "Fine, just fine."

"Well, I understand Miss Montrose only used a few rooms. She closed the rest of the house off in the last ten years or so. A house that size used to require over twenty servants to keep it in order. Nowhere would anyone get that kind of staff nowadays. Best use for it, in my opinion, is to raze it, subdivide the property, build a retirement community—townhouses, nine-hole golf course, maybe tennis courts. Just the thing for rich retirees from up north looking for a moderate climate, leisure activities. You could make a pretty penny selling it, I'll tell you."

His suggestion struck Joy like a stab wound. She was surprised at her own reaction. Desecrate a beautiful, historically rich estate? She gazed at Mr. Tedroe, barely able to conceal her horror. Did he have no sense of the past, its importance? Maybe he was just thinking like a Realtor about valuable property. She was surprised to be taking it so personally. After all, only a week ago she had not even been aware of Montclair as her inheritance. What was to become of it was now up to her. She took the floor plan from him and said good-bye as quickly as she could without being rude, then rushed out to join Gayle in the car.

By the time they shopped for groceries, stopped at the hardware store for flashlights and batteries, they got to Montclair later than they had planned.

On the way out from town Gayle remarked, "I've heard Montclair is haunted." She gave Joy a sidelong glance. "Sometimes you hear the rustle of taffeta skirts behind you on the stairs, and then there's a lady in pink who dances on the lawn with her parasol on moonlit nights, and a mysterious lady who arrives by carriage and peers in the gates, then goes away again."

"You're teasing!" Joy looked skeptical.

Gayle shook her head. "No, it's true. My grandmother told me herself that her own mother told her."

"You don't really believe that, do you?" Joy asked half seriously. "If there are any ghosts at Montclair, I'm sure they're benevolent ones. My ancestors were good people. I think it was a happy place. Ghosts haunt places that are dark and mysterious, with evil secrets like murder and that sort of stuff, right?"

"Well, I don't know about your ancestors, Joy, but my ancestors lived here, too, remember? And I'm not sure their lives were all that happy."

Joy realized that was probably true. She and Gayle were coming back to a place from different perspectives.

"I'm sorry, Gayle. I didn't think. I hope this won't be a sad experience for you."

"No, I'm really interested. It's a part of my heritage, too, you know. A part that I haven't really wanted to know about, but now I do."

The early morning sunshine was fading when they reached Montclair, and accumulated clouds again threatened rain. They unloaded their things and unlocked the front door.

It creaked a little on its hinges as they walked into the wide center hall. Both stood still for a minute as if listening for something. The house had a waiting feel but not an unwelcome one.

They dumped their belongings on the floor and looked around in awe.

"Where do we begin?" Gayle asked.

"Why don't we start by using the floor plan as a guide? Later we can decide where we'll sleep."

They took the groceries out to the kitchen, which they discovered had been added onto the house in the early 1880s, together with the pantry. Consulting the plan, they discovered that originally the kitchen and bakehouse had been in separate buildings and adjoined the house with a covered breezeway.

From there they went back through a huge dining room, pausing to look through French doors leading out onto the veranda which encircled the house. Sliding doors on either side of the entrance hall led to what were identified as twin parlors. There were only a few pieces of furniture, draped in dust cloths, but there were magnificent fireplaces with marble mantels, and over the fireplace in one of the parlors hung a huge, ornately framed mirror. The glass was discolored and showed a crack in the lower part. How many gala parties, wedding receptions, lavish soirees of all kinds had it once reflected, as the high ceilings and polished floors echoed with music and dancing? What other scenes had it imaged? Scenes of conflict, drama, sorrow, happiness—of life that had been lived by real people generation after generation.

"I know it's a cliché, but just imagine if these walls could talk," Gayle said in a voice close to a whisper.

There were two other rooms, mostly empty, which the floor plan indicated were the library and music room. Down the hallway was a room that was designated as the master bedroom. Its windows were shuttered, and when Joy opened one, she saw it looked out on the side lawn and the curve of the driveway. The only furniture was a large poster bed with pineapple finials. An open door near the bed revealed a narrow, winding staircase.

"I wonder where this leads?"

Gayle consulted the floor plan. "It says, 'To Nursery.' I believe in the olden days this stairway was provided so that the nurse could bring the baby down to the mother without going through the main part of the house."

"Shall we go up?"

"Let's use the big staircase. We can probably come back down this one."

Upstairs the second floor was laid out much like the first floor. There was a long center hall with eight bedrooms, four on either side, with smaller rooms—probably dressing rooms or sitting rooms—adjoining each.

"I wonder where the nursery is," Joy said.

"It should be at the end, I think, right over the master bedroom."

154

Again it was like entering the past when they found the nursery and tiptoed in. For a room which once must have been filled with light and the sound of lullabies and children's laughter, it seemed somehow gloomy. Generations of Joy's ancestors had played in this room, been rocked to sleep here. So why this feeling of melancholy? Joy wondered. For someone who had never known roots or family connections, it should have made her feel warm and happy.

Then Gayle said softly, "There was a high mortality rate for babies in the old days. There were no vaccines or much preventive care."

Joy knew it was the modern doctor in Gayle making the observation. Maybe Gayle might have somehow sensed the tears that might have been shed in this room over a hopelessly sick baby.

"Let's go," Joy said, moving to the door.

Gayle's voice halted her. "You know, Joy, there is supposed to be a secret room in this house. It's not in this"—she tapped the sheets of the floor plan she held—"but I once heard my grandmother telling my mother about it. I don't know why, but I never paid too much attention to her stories about the old days. I was always somewhat impatient when hearing about the Montrose family. That connection was a symbol of all we'd come so far away from. I didn't want to feel any identity, any nostalgia, about slavery. Of course, my Great-Great-Grandmother Tilda had different ties with the Montroses, and even affection for them. Especially, of course, for Miss Rose."

"A secret room?"

"Yes, and I'm trying to remember where it was. If I'm not mistaken, it was off the nursery."

"That's exciting. Let's try to find it," Joy suggested.

The walls were half paneled, with wainscoting about four feet high, and the rest wallpapered. Even though the pattern

155

was badly faded, Joy could still discern images of toys—jack-in-the-boxes, dolls, pyramids of blocks. She and Gayle began slowly circling the room, running their hands across and down where there seemed to be ridges.

Suddenly Gayle exclaimed, "Here, Joy—I think it's here!" She moved both hands down and along the ridge of the paneling. With a creaking sound, the door slid back and opened.

"Ohmigosh, we've found it!" Joy breathed.

The smell of dampness, mold, old dirt prickled their nostrils, and both leaned into the dark space.

"Did you bring the flashlight?" Gayle asked in a hushed voice.

"I'll go get it," Joy answered and ran back downstairs to the front hall, where they had dumped their belongings. She was back in two minutes, bringing both flashlights. She handed one to Gayle and flicked on hers. The circle of light beamed into the dark room, revealing a small, narrow passageway, almost a crawl space. Gingerly Joy took a few steps inside, moving her flashlight around.

"There's a door at the far end," she said over her shoulder to Gayle, who remained in the nursery but also shone her flashlight into the darkness. "And there are things stored in here!" Joy sounded excited. "I believe they're pictures. Wait, I'll see." There was a short silence, and then her voice rang out. "Gayle, they're paintings! Maybe they're the ones that were hung on the wall beside the staircase. They seem to be about the size of those faded outlines we saw in the wallpaper. I'll bring one out."

Breathing hard, Joy emerged backward, dragging a large square object wrapped in heavy brown paper and tied in several twists of twine. She propped it against the wall, then began working at the wrapping. There were several layers of paper, and the twine had been tied into several knots. "I wish I had a knife or some scissors," Joy said impatiently. At last she managed to get a large enough rip in one side, then tore the paper away. The edge of an ornate but badly tarnished frame appeared. "It is!" she cried excitedly. "It's a portrait."

Gayle began to help her tear the rest of the paper away. Then they both stepped back to see what was revealed. The canvas was thick with accumulated dust. It needed a good, expert cleaning, Joy observed, but the radiant young beauty of the subject was still visible. Abundant auburn hair piled high on a gracefully held head. Patrician features in a classically oval face. A rosebud mouth, its corners lifted in a demure smile. And a mischievous sparkle in the eyes. Who was she?

It was Gayle who saw the small brass plaque at the bottom of the frame. She bent closer, beaming the flashlight onto the engraved name. "Avril Dumont Montrose," she read out loud.

"One of the brides," said Joy.

"There's a date," Gayle said. "1816."

"Imagine!" Joy was awed. "She looks so young."

"Do you think the other portraits are also stored in there?" asked Gayle.

"They seem to be. Let's bring them out into the nursery. We can unwrap them and look at them tomorrow—after we get some scissors and some better lighting so we can examine them more closely."

Joy was excited. This was becoming a treasure hunt. No telling what else they might find in this house that had belonged to her family for generations.

After they had dragged all the portraits out and lined them along the nursery walls, Gayle and Joy went back into the room with their flashlights to check out the rest of the space. Two large cardboard boxes were pulled out. With a final sweep of their beams, they saw something shoved under the eaves.

It was a shoe box, much the worse for wear after years of storage in this unventilated place. Masking tape was wound all around the box to seal it. On top, in childish block letters, were the words "TO BE OPENED ON NEW YEAR'S DAY 1912."

"1912!" both women gasped, looking at each other.

"What in the world could be in it?" Joy wondered.

"Only one way to find out," Gayle said, smiling.

The masking tape was stiff with age, but gradually they got it off and opened the lid.

chapter

18

INSIDE THE BOX, on top of its contents, was an envelope with the words "To Whom It May Concern" written in a child's printing and signed Nicki Montrose.

Joy looked at Gayle. "That was my grandmother. Molly told me about her. She was orphaned by World War I and adopted by the Montrose family. She must have put this here."

"Well, go ahead, open it. You're entitled," Gayle said.

Breathlessly Joy picked up the envelope, slid her finger under the flap, took out a folded piece of lined notebook paper, and read it out loud.

October 1932

Scotty Cameron and I found this box that was to be opened in 1912, twenty years ago. Before we had a chance to go through all the stuff together, Scotty left for England with her mother, Jill, for a visit. We had to keep it a secret, like this room. Nobody seems to know about it but us. I haven't even told Luc.

We plan to look for other things to put in this box. There must be more here about both the Montrose and Cameron families, going back a hundred years to when Montclair, this house, was built. Scotty is related to almost everyone mentioned. I'm not. I'm really French. Tante (Cara Cameron, now Cara Montrose) adopted me when I was four, from an orphanage in France. So I don't know who I really am. That's weird. Someday I intend to go to France and find out.

Anyway, I don't know what we'll do with all this. I'm putting this in the box along with the other stuff in case we don't get back to it.

Joy peered into the box. "I guess they didn't. It looks as if everything is still here, just as two kids would leave it."

"Let's see."

One by one they brought out the items. The first was a small framed picture wrapped in tissue paper, a sepia photograph of a couple. The pretty young woman, hardly more than a girl, wore a ruffled dress and posed with one hand on the shoulder of the seated man, a handsome fellow with thick dark hair and a mustache and melancholy dark eyes. Turning it over, Joy saw the name of a photographer in Lucas Valley, California, and the date 1870.

"California!" they both exclaimed.

Joy picked up a rolled parchment tied with a faded ribbon, which when opened was a marriage certificate with the names Blythe Dorman and Malcolm Montrose. Attached to this was a note: "This is Kip's grandfather and my mother." It was signed Cara Cameron.

There were a few other things in the box that did not seem to be of much value or significance. There was a toy airplane, some stones and shells, some yellowed snapshots of twin girls and of another little girl, two blue award ribbons, perhaps won in horse shows.

Since both of them were starting to get hungry, they decided to take the two large cardboard boxes down to the kitchen and explore them there.

Joy lit a few of the candles they had purchased at the gro-cery store, and they opened the boxes. Inside were some beau-tiful pieces of china—odds and ends, not a full or matching set. There were also several fine examples of cut glass.

"These are worth a fortune, Joy," Gayle told her as she held one graceful vase in both hands. Even in the flickering candle-light and dulled by years of being packed away unused, it still had a sparkle.

They were just setting out the makeshift meal of crackers, cheese, peanut butter, fruit, and cookies when they heard a car motor outside. It stopped, and a moment later the sound of the knocker on the front door echoed through the house.

"Who could that be?" Joy murmured as she went to answer it.

A well-dressed middle-aged gentleman stood at the door. He removed his hat, displaying a head of wavy gray hair, and gave a slight bow. "Miss Montrose? I'm Jason Lawrence, the attorney who contacted you about Montclair. Mr. Tedroe told me you had come by his office, and I just wanted to bring you this." He pointed to a small, old-fashioned trunk he had set on the porch. "Miss Heather Montrose left this in my keep-ing. I believe she realized she was getting on in years and wanted it in a safe place. Over the years she had collected a great many family papers and other memorabilia that she felt would be of interest to the heir if we could locate him or her.

"She also left this." He drew a long envelope from the inside pocket of his jacket and handed it to Joy. "She hoped so much that someone would be found. Sadly, she didn't live to know about you." He lifted the little trunk and set it inside. "I'm looking forward to discussing your plans with you when you have reached a decision about what to do with Montclair." He glanced over her shoulder into the hall questioningly. "Are you here alone?"

"I have a friend with me. We're quite all right, thank you. I haven't come to any decision as yet, Mr. Lawrence, but I certainly will come by your office before I leave."

He looked rather doubtful but politely took his leave. Joy watched him go down the drive, and then she put the envelope in her sweater pocket to read later. She called Gayle to help her lug the trunk into the kitchen. Although it was small, it was quite heavy.

"I wonder if you have another treasure trove in here," Gayle said, rolling her eyes dramatically.

It was a treasure of a very different kind—the trunk was packed with scrapbooks and photograph albums.

It was an evening Joy would never forget as she turned page after page of yellowed newspaper clippings, reading of the events that had shaped the lives of her ancestors through the years. Names she had never heard now became familiar as she read of the births, engagements, weddings, deaths, and other important occasions.

Malcolm Montrose Takes Massachusetts Bride

1857

Milford, Massachusetts, was the scene today of the wedding of Miss Rose Meredith, of Milford, and Mr. Malcolm Montrose, eldest son of Mr. and Mrs. Clayborn Montrose of Montclair. Malcolm Montrose was a Harvard classmate of Miss Meredith's brother John.

1857

Two prominent Mayfield families are joined as Miss Garnet Cameron and Mr. Bryson Montrose make their vows at Montclair, the home of the groom's parents. This is the second son in the Montrose family to take a bride this summer.

1858

A son, Jonathan Meredith, was born to Mr. and Mrs. Malcolm Montrose at the family estate, Montclair. Mrs. Montrose is the former Miss Rose Meredith of Milford, Massachusetts.

1920

Lynette Montrose became the bride of newly elected state senator Frank Maynard in a private ceremony in the family chapel on the Montclair estate.

1921

Scott Cameron, editor of the local newspaper, marries Jillian Marsh at the family estate, Cameron Hall. Miss Marsh is a native of England and a distant descendant of Noramary Marsh, the first bride of Montclair, which is the estate of the Camerons' longtime friends and neighbors, the Montrose family.

1944

Mayfield mourns one of its native sons in the death of Kendall Montrose, affectionately known as Kip. An ace pilot and a member of the WWI volunteer corps the Lafayette Esquadrille, Colonel Montrose died in the crash of a B-52 bomber he was transporting from Kelly Field in Texas. He is survived by his wife, Cara (Cameron) Montrose, a son, Luc (at present a German POW), and an adopted daughter, Nicole.

A handwritten note followed, stating that the poem it quoted was read at Kendall Montrose's memorial service. The poem was attributed to John Magee, a British pilot who had been killed in action.

I have slipped the surly bonds of earth
And danced the skies on laughter's silvered wings:
Sunward I've climbed and joined the tumbling mirth
Of sunlit clouds, and done a hundred things

You have not dreamed of, wheeled and soared and swung
High in the sunlit silence, hovering there
I've chased the shouting wind along and flung
My eager craft through footless halls of air.
I've topped the windswept heights with easy grace
Where neither lark or even eagle flew.
And while, with silent lifting mind I've trod
The high untrespassed sanctuary of space
Put out my hand, and touched the face of God.

Tears blurred Joy's eyes as she read. Surely this poem could have been read also at her father's military funeral. She had no idea what that ceremony had been like for her young mother, who, like Cara Montrose, had suddenly and tragically become a pilot's widow.

Joy read on, thinking how many hours Heather Montrose must have spent putting all this together, not even sure anyone else would ever see these pages.

Senior Citizen Takes Unusual Step

1951

Sixty-year-old resident Cara Cameron Montrose has joined the Peace Corps. When interviewed, Mrs. Montrose, who served as a Red Cross ambulance driver in WWI and again as a counselor in army hospitals in WWII, told this reporter, "I feel my experience and training can make a contribution in a work I believe is worthwhile and rewarding."

Local Author Opens Ancestral Home

May 1954

Nora Scott Cameron, who is known to family and friends as Scotty and is well known among regional southern writers, has opened her family home, Cameron Hall, for the Christmas season house tour. Miss Cameron divides her time between

Virginia and rural England, where her mother, the former Jillian Marsh, widow of Scott Cameron, the late editor of the *Mayfield Monitor,* lives in a picturesque thatched-roof home called Larkspur Cottage. Miss Cameron is the author of a multivolume history of the Mayfield area.

Stewart Cameron, a recently ordained minister and son of the late Scott Cameron, former editor of the *Mayfield Monitor,* has taken the position of rector at Mayfield's Episcopal church, St. Luke the Physician. He and his wife, the former Fiona Montrose, and their two small children will take up residence in Mayfield after a visit to Scotland, Mrs. Cameron's native country.

Suddenly Joy came across this headline from the *Mayfield Monitor:*

Local Man Casualty in Vietnam

April 1968

Lt. Beaumont Montrose, a helicopter pilot and the only son of Mr. and Mrs. Fraser Montrose of Montclair, was killed last week, it was learned.

The father she had never known! Here in Mayfield he had been well known, loved, missed. What had he been like, this young naval lieutenant who had married Anne Layton in a whirlwind courtship and had never been able to bring his bride home to Montclair? Joy could only imagine the love that had come to these two young people who had been her parents, a love that had so tragically ended.

Model Discovered in Unlikely Place

1972

A mystery in the world of high fashion has at last been solved. Natasha Oblenskova, beautiful French-born model, disappeared from the fashion scene two years ago. Efforts to discover her location failed. Neither her agent nor the model agency that had managed her career would give any comments or information. Recently it was learned from reliable sources that the glamorous young woman, whose image had appeared numerous times on such magazines as *Vogue, Harper's Bazaar, Elle,* and *WW,* has taken vows to join a Russian Orthodox order of nuns. The cloistered convent is located in Connecticut, where Miss Oblenskova grew up with her mother, the former Evalee Bondurant, and her stepfather, Alan Reid. Miss Oblenskova is the granddaughter of Mrs. Druscilla Montrose Bondurant of Mayfield, Virginia.

1973

Hope Montrose, the famous illustrator of children's books, both new and classics, will be signing her latest at the Abordale Library next Thursday from two until four. Ms. Montrose is currently visiting Avalon, her childhood home. Ms. Montrose is the daughter of Gareth and the late Brooke Montrose, and the granddaughter of the internationally known artist Jeff Montrose.

Fabulous Antique Jewelry Donated to Smithsonian

A set consisting of a ruby-and-diamond necklace and matching earrings, which is believed to be the work of an eighteenth-century designer to royalty and which had been in the Montrose family for generations, was presented to the curators of the Washington, D.C., institution. It was originally created for and given to Claire Fraser, the first Montrose bride and for whom Montclair was built.

Cara-Lyn Maynard, daughter of state senator Frank Maynard and his wife, the former Lynette Montrose, was recently decorated by the president for extraordinary valor in her work as a photographer in Korea. She is one of few women so honored.

At the very bottom of the trunk were several books. One was a Bible, its leather cover blistered as if by fire, the edges of the pages scorched, on which was embossed, in gold letters so tarnished that they were barely discernible, the name Rose Meredith Montrose. There was a worn copy of Tennyson's *Idylls of the King,* with this inscription:

> *To my dear son Malcolm—a real knight in shining armor,*
>> *from your loving mother,*
>> *Sara Leighton Montrose*

A verse within had been heavily underlined.

More things are wrought by prayer than this world little dreams of.

Joy picked up a battered New Testament that had apparently belonged to Malcolm Montrose. It looked as though it had been through a war—and probably had. Inside was a poem, written in ink that had turned a faint brown. A note in the margin identified the author as an anonymous Confederate soldier.

I asked God for strength, that I might achieve,
I was made weak, that I might learn humbly to obey,
I asked for health that I might do greater things,
I was given infirmity that I might do better things.
I asked for riches that I might be happy,
I was given poverty, that I might be wise.
I asked for power, that I might have the praise of men.
I was given weakness, that I might feel the need of God.
I asked for all things that I might enjoy life.
I was given life that I might enjoy all things.
I got nothing that I asked for—but everything I had hoped for.
Almost despite myself, my unspoken prayers were answered.
I am among all men, most richly blessed.

Malcolm must have copied it.

There were two books wrapped together. One was a book of poetry entitled *POEMS, 1916–1918* by Richard Traherne;

the other was *No Cheers, No Glory: A True Account of a Field Nurse in Wartime France* by Katherine Cameron Traherne. The dates on some of the pages were closer to the one Joy was most interested in finding. She was seeking some word about her father, the Montrose she had never known. Here in Mayfield he had a family, a whole life, that she knew nothing about. She turned a page and suddenly saw something that made her heart jump.

New Arrival in Mayfield

Mr. and Mrs. Fraser Montrose welcome a son, christened Beaumont. He joins his sister, Heather, at the family home, Montclair.

Gayle, rolled up in her sleeping bag, had finally succumbed to sleep, but Joy was not tired. Too much was unfolding here. People, events, stories she had never heard of nor imagined. It was like reading a fascinating novel, but it was real—and all these things had happened to her relatives.

Had her grandmother Nicole ever returned to France, as was her childhood dream? Had she made that search for her real parents? Had she found them? And if so, who were they? Missing parts of the puzzle of her own background. Whom had her father been named after? Beaumont Montrose sounded sort of French. "Beau," his nickname, made him seem dashing, adventurous, reckless. From the one photograph she had seen of him—leaning against his helicopter, wearing a leather flight jacket, his uniform hat jauntily askew—he was certainly handsome.

The candle was burning low, the flame flickering, and yet, driven by the need to know more, Joy kept turning the pages, reading the items her aunt, Heather Montrose, had so painstakingly cut out and organized, hoping that some future unknown kin would find them interesting and important. The photographs were equally of interest. There was one labeled "Cape Cod, Summer 1909" and filled with groups of smiling young people, all neatly identified with white ink on the black plates. As Joy looked at it, she recognized some of the names, such as Kip and Cara. She wondered who the others were—Kitty, Hugh, Owen, Meredith—and what had happened to them since that carefree summer long ago.

Joy closed the trunk. This trip into the past—peopled by so many who had lived under this roof, gone from here to wars, come to this house as brides—had been both exhilarating and exhausting. She felt drained and yet eager to learn more. Her eyelids drooped, and she blew out the sputtering candle and climbed into her sleeping bag. All at once she remembered the envelope she had stuffed into her sweater and then in the excitement of emptying the trunk had forgotten. She was too tired now. Tomorrow there would be time enough to read it.

When Joy awoke on Sunday, the sun was streaming in through the windows. They had pushed back the inside shutters the night before. Gayle's sleeping bag was empty, and when Joy got up, she saw a note on the table: "It's such a beautiful day, I've gone exploring." Joy slipped on her jeans and grabbed an orange from the bag they had bought the day before and hurried outside. The air was fresh from the rain, and Joy breathed deeply, thinking of the many other Montrose women who had stood on this same porch and seen the sweep of land called Montclair.

Soon Joy saw Gayle coming toward her from the woods beyond the meadow. She waved and called something, and Joy hastened to join her.

"Guess what I've found?" Gayle said when Joy approached. "A family cemetery. It's terribly overgrown, but I peeked through the fence and there are several headstones, all probably belonging to your ancestors." She paused. "There's another graveyard a little apart, with a sign I could barely make out. I think it said, 'Our People'—it must mean the slaves are buried there."

"Shall we go take a look?" suggested Joy, not sure it was the right thing to ask her. But Gayle agreed, and together they retraced her steps up the path that wound up the hillside.

It took both of them to push back the iron gate and enter the cemetery. The grass was high. Blackberry bushes had invaded the plot, so they had to pick their way through them to examine the names on the headstones. They moved silently, stopping here and there to read a name, a date. It seemed the last one buried here was Malcolm Montrose. His grave was next to one marked "Rose Meredith Montrose, Beloved Wife of Malcolm."

In quiet agreement they left the Montrose burial grounds, pulling the gate closed behind them. Together they walked a few yards further and found the sign that marked the opening to the other graveyard. Here wooden crosses marched in staggered lines, row after row. On the crossbars were simply carved first names: "Mom Becca," "Lonnie," "Big Jim," "Joshua," "Ellie." The two young women did not speak as they wandered through the cemetery, each wrapped in her own thoughts. The humble resting place seemed somehow to lend some dignity to a dark, unhappy time in American history.

"I should see that these are tended to regularly. It is sacred ground," was Joy's only comment as they left and walked back down the hill to the house.

They decided to drive into town to find a church and attend services. Down the road from Montclair they saw a small, white frame church building. Gayle slowed the car. "Here?"

"Why not?" Joy responded.

As they entered, a choir in bright blue robes was singing "Shine, Jesus, Shine." They smiled in recognition of the lively hymn and found places in a back pew and joined in.

Despite the uplifting service, Gayle was unusually quiet for the rest of the day as they continued to explore Montclair. Joy sensed that the walk through the slave cemetery had affected her deeply. She realized that Gayle needed time to absorb this face-to-face confrontation with her past and reconcile it somehow to her own life.

On Monday Joy had an appointment with Mr. Lawrence in town. Gayle dropped her off at the lawyer's office, saying she thought she would go to the local library and do a little research about Mayfield on her own. They would meet in about an hour.

The discussion with the lawyer proved both instructive and helpful. Mr. Lawrence was a gracious, kindly person with all the legendary courtesy of a southern gentleman. When Joy pointed out that she was single and had a career and that there was not the slightest possibility that she would ever take possession of and live at Montclair, he suggested an alternative.

"The Mayfield Historical Society has long been interested in Montclair. It was one of the first plantations built on the James River, an original king's grant to the Montrose family when they came here from Scotland. It is a treasure, and I know they have been worried that, unoccupied, it would soon fall into a state of such deterioration that it would be too costly to restore. If you deeded it to them, it would minimize your tax responsibility to an enormous extent and preserve its historic value. I am sure they would want most of the furnishings as well. Of course, you could pick which items you wanted personally. The house would then be made open to tourists, after being restored as closely as possible to the state it was in when it was not only a working plantation but a home known for its hospitality. All this could be arranged legally to give you the most benefit and yet be a wonderful gift to the community."

"I have a lot to think about, Mr. Lawrence. Thank you for all your help."

"It has been my pleasure, and I stand ready to assist you in any way. I was very fond of Miss Montrose. I feel that deeding Montclair to the historical society would be very acceptable to her." He paused. "Perhaps that may have even been her own suggestion in her letter?"

It was only then that Joy realized she had not yet read it. She was embarrassed to admit it, so she just said, "There is a great deal to consider. I want to do the right thing." She moved to the door. "I'll be in touch, Mr. Lawrence, and thank you again."

"Mayfield has a checkered history," Gayle told her when they met. "For a small town, it has had a dramatic life. I only got up to the 1790s!"

"The past seems so real and so close here, doesn't it?" Joy asked as they left town and started back to Montclair.

"Too close at times. I told you my grandmother said Montclair was haunted," Gayle reminded her with a rueful smile.

When they got to Montclair, Gayle said she was going to take a long walk. Joy sensed that she wanted to go alone, so they parted. Joy went into the house. This would be a good time to read the letter Heather Montrose had left for her.

chapter
19

Dear Whoever You Are,

If you are reading this, I assume my lawyers have ended their search successfully and you are now at Montclair. I hope you will stay a few days or longer. Even if you have simply come through the front door, I trust you will feel that sense of awe upon entering.

A house where generations of your family were born, grew up, lived, left, and then returned has a unique quality. It gives one the sense of continuity, a feeling of belonging that is rare and unique. The echo of footsteps on the stairs or in the halls is not disturbing but affirming. It gives one the foundation of security, a peace that neither time nor personal loss nor even sorrow can take away.

Although I now live here alone, the tide of life that flows through Montclair is tangible. A house holds all that has been lived and experienced within it down through the years. Even though all that makes up human existence has been played out here, it is not an unhappy place. I have never felt lonely here. As I grew older, I felt it was important to leave something for whoever came after me, so I've assembled the scrapbooks, a collection of as much information as I could gather about those who have called Montclair home.

In my earliest memories of Montclair, it is as if the sun were always shining. I remember warm days playing on the velvety grass around the house in my bare feet with my cousins Hope—daughter of my uncle Gareth and his beautiful wife, Brooke—and Hugh and Honor Cameron. We would play on the swings under the leafy oaks, ride our ponies, and catch fireflies on summer evenings while the grown-ups sat on the veranda, from which we could hear the murmur of their low voices, occasionally punctuated by light laughter.

What I discovered on my own about this place is that you can go away, but you take Montclair with you. When I was ten, I contracted polio in the days before the wonderful Salk vaccine made this parents' nightmare virtually extinct. I recovered, but my health was afterward fragile, and my mother, Nicole, took me to various clinics and health resorts to see if my constitution could be strengthened and restored. This often meant travel abroad, and we were gone for months sometimes. I was often homesick and missed my adored father, Fraser Montrose, very much.

It wasn't until I was older that I learned that besides seeking health for me, my mother was on a quest of her own. Orphaned after the First World War, she was adopted by Cara Cameron Montrose and brought to the United States, to Mayfield and Montclair. But as with many orphans, there was always this hunger within her to find out about her real parents and background. Thus we traveled widely throughout France, following one clue after another.

But this is another story altogether. My mother never told it. However, I believe that the name of my little brother, Beaumont, who was born after one of our trips, had something to do with one of her discoveries. I vaguely remember a picturesque village and a chateau we visited in which my mother had long conversations with an elderly woman who had been the housekeeper for the family who had lived there.

Moving from this personal vein, Heather's letter went on to note some of the history of the house, how it had been built for one bride, but when she eloped with someone else before the wedding, her cousin had become a substitute bride and the first mistress. The additions were explained, such as the balcony added for the invalid Sara, injured in a horseback-riding accident. Her letter recounted the times Montclair had hosted the governor of the state, and mentioned other dignitaries who had enjoyed its legendary hospitality.

A fact that intrigued Joy was the mention of Eden Cottage, the architect's model of Montclair built about three miles from the main house. It became traditionally the place where the eldest son and his bride spent their honeymoon year. She would like to try to find it if it still existed.

The letter ended with two poignant paragraphs:

> *I sense that you somehow had no idea of your connection with the Montroses of Mayfield, Virginia, or you would have made yourself known before this. My younger brother Beaumont and I, as the children of Fraser and Nicole Montrose, jointly inherited Montclair. However, after Beaumont was killed, his widow never made contact with our family. All we knew was that they were expecting a baby. My lawyers have been searching for that child over the past few years. Since I never married or had any children, you are the sole heir.*
>
> *I have to assume inheriting Montclair will come as a shock to you. I have no idea if you are male or female, married with a family or single. I can only say you are now the possessor of a splendid legacy that goes back to prerevolutionary Virginia, when our ancestor Duncan Montrose cleared the property on the James River and built Montclair.*
>
> *I give you permission to take any of the furnishings, the silver, the china, or crystal that is in the house for your own.*

In this day and age, maintaining a house this large and the land would require a great deal of money. I have told my lawyers that if their search for the heir to Montclair proved fruitless within five years after my death, it is my wish that the house should be donated to the Mayfield Historical Society. As much land should be sold as needed to pay the back taxes that will have accumulated, so they can take over the property without heavy liens against it. All this can be worked out legally in due time.

Even though I will never know you, I feel a kinship with you as you read this—and a hope for the future. Somehow I feel that the splendid legacy of Montclair will escape the ruthless onslaught of so-called progress and never be turned into a country club or torn down to make room for a condominium complex but will remain as a symbol of its significant historical importance for generations to come.

Heather Montrose

Joy finished reading the letter. Her questions had not all been answered by everything Heather had left behind, and maybe the mysteries would remain forever. She would have to be satisfied with that. Heather Montrose had done her best to give Joy an idea of her background. Even with the loopholes that remained, Joy could understand how her young mother, grief-stricken and pregnant, had not contacted her husband's family. They had not known there was a grandchild expected, and shortly afterward both had died. Heather, the only remaining member of the family, had tried to fill in the gaps.

Joy now felt more confident about what to do. No longer did she feel so completely overwhelmed by her unexpected inheritance. Heather had given her direction.

chapter
20

THE MORNING THEY were to leave Montclair, both Joy and Gayle were singularly quiet, as if caught up in the ambiance of the past, the aura of their surroundings. They had stayed up late packing a few things Joy decided to take back with her.

After they finished their cups of instant coffee, Gayle put on her jacket. "I think I'll walk back to the cemetery again. There are some early daffodils blooming along the drive—is it okay if I pick some to take up there?"

"Of course," Joy assured her. She picked up her canvas tote bag and said, "I'm going to take a last walk through the house."

After Gayle left, Joy went out into the center hall, then slowly mounted the stairway. She glanced at the squares of less-faded wallpaper that had been left when the brides' portraits were taken down. The restorers would probably try to match the pattern, and the paintings would be rehung. It gave Joy a deep sense of satisfaction to know that deeding Montclair to the preservation group would bring it back to its former glory. Then the women who had been mistresses here would again smile from their places of honor.

Upstairs, she walked the length of the hallway, stopping to open bedroom doors, pausing on a threshold or taking a few steps inside to admire a fireplace or check the view from a window. In the nursery she lingered. Her special fondness for this room because of the discoveries they had made there had grown after reading what Heather had written in her letter:

There is supposed to be a hidden room in Montclair, but no one I ever knew found it. There are rumors that this was once a "safe house" in the Underground Railroad, to shelter runaway slaves escaping to the North. But nothing ever proved that to be true.

Joy smiled. Heather's mother, the Nicki of the note in the shoe box, must have kept her and Scotty Cameron's find a secret, even from her daughter.

Reluctantly Joy ended her tour of the second floor and went back downstairs. She wandered through the library, whose bookshelves were nearly emptied. Heather had mentioned in her letter that she had given boxes of books to the local library, and some valued first editions to the Mayfield museum. All that identified the music room were a bust of Beethoven and one of Mozart, both on pedestals. Any instruments must have long since been removed. She passed the twin parlors to go further down the hall to the master bedroom suite. She circled the room, touching the handsome rosewood furniture, the high bed with its carved pineapple posters, the drop-leaf table and two Queen Anne chairs set in the bow-windowed alcove. She lingered at the magnificent bureau.

For some reason she took hold of the carved-leaf drawer pulls and one by one opened the drawers. She caught the faint fragrance of crushed roses. She imagined that long ago fragrant dried petals in tiny net-wrapped sachets were spread among ruffled petticoats and camisoles. She closed the last drawer—and then, quite inadvertently, her foot touched the ornamental base of the bureau. With a click it fell forward, revealing a concealed shelf. A secret compartment! Joy crouched down to examine it and saw something inside. A thin, leather-bound book. She reached in her hand and drew it out. The cover was dusty, the gilded pages tarnished. Gingerly she opened it. On the flyleaf was written, with fine Spencerian hand in faded ink, "Rose Meredith Montrose. Journal 1861–1862."

Joy's heart began to thump. Carefully she turned the first page. The script was so tightly spaced, it was difficult to read.

> *If I didn't have this journal to pour out my feelings, I do not know what I would do. I am so miserable and feel so guilty. How could I be so unhappy in such beautiful sur-roundings, such luxurious circumstances? And yet not so long ago I thought myself the happiest of women.*
>
> *I now look back on the first year of our marriage, spent in Eden Cottage, as idyllic. Not a cross word ever spoken between us, not the slightest unpleasant moment. But was I simply blinded by love? Had I not heeded what Kendall Carpenter tried to point out to me in his impassioned pleas and what even my dear brother John more cautiously put forward for me to consider—that Malcolm and I came from far different spiritual and philosophical and cultural backgrounds? Did I choose to ignore that we might have been "unequally yoked" even from the first?*

Joy almost closed the book and replaced it. This was like looking into someone's open heart. These words were not meant for anyone else's eyes. And yet she could not bear to put it back, to stop reading.

> *Malcolm is gone and I am devastated. We parted in anger. I fear the chasm between us is too wide and deep to ever be bridged. I am so unhappy. I wish I could call back all my words and had not heard his. Things will never be*

the same, and now it is too late to remedy the breech, too late to ask forgiveness or to forgive.

I feel so lonely, so afraid. My life is in ruins. My darling Malcolm gone fighting in this horrible war, and my brother John fighting against him on the other side. I know John has chosen the right. Slavery is wrong and should be ended. In his heart I believe Malcolm knows this, but he said he cannot go against his heritage, his state.

Between these anguished entries Rose had copied Scripture verses, as if she sought reassurance and strength. Some of the writing was blurred, as if tears had dropped on the pages as she wrote.

Joy sat down on the floor, unable to stop reading. It was a compelling narrative, as absorbing as any historical novel.

I am alone here with Mother-in-Law Sara. She is as demanding as ever, even more so now that Lizzie has disappeared. If she ever knew I had any part in that, I don't know what the consequences would be. Garnet is in Richmond. So I hold the fort here. Of course, the servants are here and Tilda is a great help with Jonathan, as I must be at Sara's beck and call. We don't get a great deal of news about the war, but what we do get is bad. Father-in-Law is very morose, worried about his sons. And so am I, dreadfully so, because my heart is divided.

Joy was compelled to continue reading. As she turned the pages, a thin sheet of paper slipped out. It was a letter. She unfolded it and read,

Beloved,

How often I have thought of you and regretted dearly the way we parted.

Her heart tripped. This was a letter from the husband about whom Rose was so grieved. Her eyes raced along the closely written lines, down the pages, then paused to read this sentence:

Let us take our marriage vows again—from this day forward to love, cherish each other until death us do part.

Breathlessly Joy turned back to the diary to read Rose's ecstatic response to the receipt of that letter.

God is so faithful. All my prayers have been answered. My dearest Malcolm has written me a precious letter. It is a priceless confirmation of the love we have for each other. Nothing can come between us, nothing can separate us, for our hearts and souls are bound to each other forever. We both want to renew our wedding promises. "What God has bound together, let no man put asunder." Amen to that.

The entries were few and far between after that. Short notations of everyday events. The rest of the pages were blank, as if the journal had suddenly halted. Had Rose merely stopped writing? Or had something caused the diary's abrupt ending?

Gayle's voice jolted Joy back to the present. She scrambled to her feet, dropping the diary into her tote bag, and hurried out into the hall. She leaned over the banister. "I'll be right down!" she called to Gayle, who was standing at the bottom of the curved stairway, looking up at her.

"You'll be happy to know I left flowers on each of the graves—in both cemeteries," Gayle told her.

"Good," Joy said. She remembered reading Rose's epitaph: "Love Is As Strong As Death." Then she suddenly recalled that the date on the headstone, 1862, was the same year as that last diary entry. Joy felt a kind of bittersweet sadness, almost as if she had known Rose. Had she died happy, anticipating a joyous reunion with her estranged husband? Joy hoped so.

181

"Are you about ready to go?" Gayle asked. "I think we should probably leave by noon. But first I want to show you something I found."

Joy followed Gayle down the drive, past the meadow on one side and an orchard with gnarled old apple trees on the other, onto a woodland path. Gayle led the way and over her shoulder told Joy, "I came down from the cemetery by another way and just happened on this." She stopped and pointed across an arched, rustic bridge. Through the thick foliage Joy saw the slanting roof of a small house. Another secret of Montclair? Could this be the Eden Cottage both Heather and Rose had mentioned? Joy felt a tingle of anticipation as they went along the path, which was almost obscured with wildflowers. When they reached a clearing, there stood a replica of Montclair. Its dimensions were cottage-size, but the architectural details were the same. It was built of clapboard and mellowed brick, with dormer windows along the second level. Two longer, shuttered windows flanked the paneled front door, which had probably once been painted bright blue.

"What do you suppose this is?"

"I know what it is. It's a honeymoon house, Eden Cottage," Joy answered and went on to explain what she had learned.

"Perfect, isn't it?" Gayle glanced at Joy. "I would consider not selling this along with the rest of the property, Joy. This would be an ideal place for you to live eventually. An artist's retreat." Then she smiled, her eyes mischievous. "Of course, you could also use it for its original purpose!"

chapter

21

As THEY CROSSED the Virginia state line, Joy felt a kind of sweet sadness, even though she knew she would be coming back again when the final papers were drawn to transfer Montclair to the Mayfield Historical Society. She planned to bring Molly with her then. Molly would love and appreciate everything. However, this first time of discovery was bittersweet and would never be repeated. Joy was leaving with a lingering memory of something priceless and special.

They got back late that afternoon. Spring had not yet arrived in this northern climate. They drove through a heavy mist that was fast turning to an icy rain. They had not talked much on the trip. Both had much to think about. Now only the whisper of the windshield wipers broke the silence that had fallen between them.

When Gayle let Joy out of the car at her tree house, she refused the offer to come in for supper. "Thanks anyway, but I have to be at the hospital early in the morning."

Joy said, "It meant so much to me for you to go with me, Gayle."

"It was good for me too, Joy. I took lots of pictures. I think my mother and grandmother will be real interested in seeing what Montclair looks like. When they're developed, I'll give you prints."

They said good-bye and Gayle drove off.

The apartment seemed damp and lonely when Joy walked inside. She dumped her suitcase and sleeping bag and went straight to the kitchen. She put the kettle on to boil water for tea. Everything seemed strange and small after the high-ceilinged, spacious rooms of Montclair.

Waiting for the tea to brew, she unzipped her tote bag and pulled out Rose's diary. She had only had time to read a few pages when she found it. Now she felt a compulsion to read more to pull this love story together, because it contained all the romantic drama, intensity, and heartbreak of a best-seller. Joy was an ardent believer that nothing happened by chance. Somehow, finding the hidden journal made it seem meant for her. She had something to learn from it. Maybe she would discover a clue to her own dilemma.

I realize now I didn't really understand about love, didn't know the real meaning of love for a lifetime, never fully grasped the depth of the vows I took. I thought I loved Malcolm with all my being. But all of him? His mind, the way he thinks, what motivates him, what his views on the important things of life are?

In my father's house I was treated as if I had some intelligence, some opinions worth expressing, and was allowed to do so. Here women are expected only to be decorative, charming, to smile and agree with everything the men believe and say. I find this difficult, and as a result Malcolm finds me difficult!

Did I make a terrible mistake in marrying Malcolm? Was it a mistake for him as well, to have a bride who doesn't quite fit the mold of a southern lady? Is love enough for us to overcome these differences? I pray so because I love Malcolm with all my passionate heart and I want us to be happy. If being myself makes him unhappy, then I was wrong to accept his proposal. It was my own weakness to love and not count the cost. I read this somewhere and copy it here: "Love's door has two keys: one is trust, that frees you to unlock that portion of yourself you must surrender to another person if you want to be loved fully; the other is hope, that the other person will allow you to love him and will love you in return."

Joy put aside the book. There was so much wisdom here. Love made life so complicated. Rose's self-questioning mirrored her own. Had Rose and Malcolm ever solved all the things that divided them, and lived happily ever after? No, not according to the date on the headstone.

As Joy sleepily got ready for bed, Rose's repeated reference to being unequally yoked lingered in her mind, as if echoing from the pages of the one-hundred-year-old diary.

The next morning when her alarm went off, Joy could hardly drag herself up and out of bed. It had snowed during the night, and a glance at the leaden sky full of heavy clouds promised they were in for a late-winter storm.

The last thing she wanted to do was brave the weather, go to the hospital, and work. Most of all, she wasn't ready to see Evan. She needed time to sort out her accumulated feelings about the weekend—and especially her feelings about him.

Coward! she accused herself. Evan would have to be faced, their relationship confronted. To heighten her tension, her car wouldn't start. Evidently, from the days of idleness the battery had run down. After several futile attempts to get the engine to turn over, Joy gave up in frustration and trudged to the bus stop.

Her stomach was tight with anxiety. She dreaded the thought of seeing Evan. As she stepped off the elevator, the possibility of that happening anytime soon vanished. The fourth floor was a scene of frantic activity. A kind of organized chaos seemed to be in progress.

From one of the haggard residents drinking coffee in the staff lounge, Joy learned that there had been a bad accident on the freeway in the early hours and that the three operating rooms and the recovery rooms were full of victims.

"A busload of skiers coming back from a mountain resort collided with a truck trailer," he told her wearily. "Those of us on the night shift have worked right on through, and every doctor on staff was called in. It's been a nightmare."

Evan would be among those called in, Joy knew. There would be no chance of seeing him for hours. She felt relieved, then suddenly guilty for thinking so selfishly.

She went into the solarium and looked at the panels but soon decided that with all the pandemonium, there was no way she could do any concentrated work. Besides, she had a headache and a stuffy nose. Maybe she was coming down with a cold. She had better go home and head it off with hot lemonade and rest.

She walked out of the hospital and into a drizzle that by the time she reached the bus stop had turned into a steady rain. Despite the shelter's protection, the wind-driven rain slashed into her mercilessly. Finally the bus lumbered up, but by the time Joy got off and ran the few blocks to her house, she was thoroughly chilled and shivering wet.

A hot bath was all she could think of. She ran a tub, poured in capfuls of scented bath oil, and eased herself into the fragrant steam. Leaning her head back on the rim of the tub, she closed her eyes and allowed herself the luxury of escape. As she relaxed in the scented warmth, as if from a long distance away she heard her phone ring. It startled her with its persistence. She did not budge, telling herself that by the time she got out of the tub, wrapped herself in a towel, it would stop. She leaned back, closed her eyes again. It rang several more times. She ignored it. Finally it stopped.

If it was Evan . . . She'd cross that bridge soon enough. She couldn't avoid him forever.

The following morning Joy went to the hospital and checked the physicians' schedule at the nurses' station. She saw that Evan had left that morning after a five-hour surgical procedure and wasn't expected back until evening rounds. That gave her some time.

She went to the solarium, intending to work on the mural. She had one miracle remaining to paint. The blind man. She still had not found the right model. She had outlined a composite figure of the man, but that was all. She stared at the unfinished panel blankly. For the second time since she had begun the mural, she felt blocked, uninspired. Joy seemed to have lost her momentum since she had been away. She knew it was mainly because she was unfocused, distracted by her uncertainty about her relationship with Evan.

She recalled Ginny Stratton telling her how helpful Sister Mary Hope had been when she was trying to break up with the married doctor. Now that the sale of the Montrose property insured that Joy could take her trip to Europe—and even stay there longer than she had ever hoped she would be able to afford—she didn't want anything to keep her from going. Falling in love had not been in her plan. It would be good to talk to someone about the conflict she had about Evan's love and her own dreams.

She knew Molly had said to pray, but she needed advice as well as divine guidance. She also needed to talk to someone who knew Evan. Sister Mary Hope was the logical person. Yes, she needed to speak with her.

Joy left the solarium and went down to the second floor. She knocked at the office of the chaplain.

Sister Mary Hope greeted Joy with a warm, assured smile, invited her to sit down in her cozy office, and offered her some tea.

Stumbling a little at first, Joy finally confided the situation, her own doubts and fears. "Evan says he loves me, and I do have a great deal of feeling for him. I just don't know if it's really love or if it's strong enough for the commitment he wants me to make."

The nun listened sympathetically, nodding understandingly as Joy poured out her feelings. It crossed Joy's mind that Sister Mary Hope may have also been in love at some time herself. She was certainly young and attractive enough.

Finally Sister Mary Hope said, "I'm glad I've seen your work, Joy, so I can fully appreciate how important it is to you. You are very talented." She paused. "A dream is a hard thing to let go of, and you've evidently had this one for a very long time." The woman regarded Joy thoughtfully. "To let go of a dream may be easier than relinquishing a real possibility. But you've been around a hospital long enough to realize how demanding a doctor's life is and the toll it must take on their families—while an artist is largely responsible only to himself or herself. Am I getting to the core of what is keeping you from accepting Dr. Wallace's proposal?"

"Yes, I think so. I feel so mixed up about it."

Sister Mary Hope smiled. "That's natural, my dear. You're still very young and have a great deal of life ahead of you. I believe love is giving yourself to somebody, really giving and caring for that person more than for yourself. It means being concerned with the other person first, before yourself. Until you honestly feel you can do that, it is better to wait."

Joy wished she could write all that down and hoped she would remember it when she talked to Evan.

Sister Mary Hope's phone rang, and she excused herself to answer it. When she put down the receiver, she apologized. "I'm sorry, Joy; I have to go. I'm needed in the ward. I hope our talk has helped a little. Please feel free to come again if you'd like."

They walked out together and Joy thanked her. It had helped but Joy wasn't quite sure how. She did feel less agitated at the thought of seeing Evan. Maybe she could explain it so he could understand that the time for them wasn't now. While he had met his goals, she still had to test her wings. There was a wide gap between where they each were in life. Maybe it was necessary for her to hold on to her dream even if it was only a stopping place on a longer journey to a more permanent destination, a place in life that she could not yet foresee.

Joy wandered back into the solarium. She didn't really feel like painting, but she knew she should start working on the painting of the blind man. Checking her notebook, she recalled that she had planned to give this scene a background of stately cedars, since after regaining his sight, the man had thought that other men were trees walking. She made a few halfhearted attempts at drawing some rough sketches of the trees, but they turned out mostly to be meaningless doodles, so she gave up and decided she was too distracted to create anything worthwhile. To her surprise it was already getting dark outside. She couldn't figure out where the afternoon had gone.

Joy stepped out from the warmth of the hospital into the early evening. More snow had fallen during the afternoon, drifting over the benches and settling onto the lampposts that lined the streets. The air was cold and there was an expectancy in it. She shivered a little, recognizing the feeling. She had it sometimes, as though something were about to happen.

Then she saw Evan's car. He tapped the horn lightly, and she realized he had been waiting for her.

"Hello, Joy," was his curt greeting when she came over to the car and he rolled down his window. "Get in, I'll drive you home. We need to talk. Your phone has a funny habit of not being answered. Maybe you'd better check with the phone company."

Evan pulled out of his parking space. They made the short distance in silence. He braked in the usual place under the tree in front of the circular staircase. He turned off the ignition and turned toward Joy, reached for her hand.

"I've been through about a half-dozen scenarios since you left. I can't tell you how it felt to get back here from the conference and not be able to see or even call you. I know I'm in love with you, Joy. I don't know why that should bother you so much, unless you aren't sure I really love you." His fingers tightened on her hand. "So one of the possibilities might be that I've been married before. Maybe that troubles you. So I wanted to be sure you understood about Susan, that I'm not still mourning her, nor am I looking for a substitute for what I've lost." He paused. "Our marriage was wonderful, unique in its own way. We were both young, ambitious, focused on our careers. Now it's over. It happened in the past. When I remember it now, it's only with gratitude for what it meant for a brief time in my life. There is no sadness that should—or would—shadow the future, our future."

Joy did not know what to say. Evan's next words made anything she might have said unnecessary.

"If I came on too strong, too soon, I'm sorry. I promise not to pressure you or rush you into any decision. Until you're ready to change things between us, can't we go on as we have?" He pressed her hand. "Well, that's all I had to say. It's up to you where we go from here. Okay?"

"I'm going to France, Evan. Alone. I don't know how long I'll stay. I can't make any promises."

"I hear what you're saying and I'm trying to understand. Letting you go scares me." He paused. "But I'm willing to play by your rules. I just don't want to lose you, Joy."

She looked into the eyes that were so full of tenderness and caring, filled with such hope and longing, and her heart melted. She wished she could say what he wanted to hear, but she couldn't. She didn't know what her future held or if Evan would be in it. All she really knew was she couldn't give up her dream.

Evan walked up the steps with her to the little balcony, held out his hand for her key, and unlocked the door. When he handed it back, he leaned down and kissed her.

"I love you, Joy."

She returned his kiss and started to say, "I love you, too." But she stopped herself. It would only make things harder for both of them. So she just murmured, "Thank you, Evan." And he turned and left.

Exhausted by her emotional day and still tired from the long trip, Joy fell asleep without eating. Her alarm was buzzing wildly when she finally woke up. It was only at the last minute that she remembered that her car was still not functioning. She had to run to catch a bus so she was late getting to the hospital.

She decided to stop in pediatrics before going up to fourth to see if Gayle could meet her for lunch. She had a great deal to talk to her about.

The minute she stepped off the elevator, she felt something was wrong. The ward was bustling with a kind of hushed activity. She saw the group of doctors and nurses clustered in consultation outside one of the rooms. Was that Debbie's room? Slowly a cold certainty washed over her. Joy was frozen to the spot. She recognized one of the doctors as Dr. Broadman, head of pediatrics. A man in his late fifties, he had been a pediatrician for years. He must have had many patients die. Yet he looked stricken.

Then she saw Gayle. At the sound of the elevator's closing doors, she turned. Her face was drawn, her expression blank. She did not even acknowledge Joy.

Joy remembered Jean Braden saying, "No one gets used to a child's dying. It's unnatural somehow. No matter how sick they were. No matter how long you've been in practice." She recalled Jean's concern about Gayle not accepting that inevitability in some cases.

Joy felt tears rush up into her own eyes. What Gayle was experiencing couldn't be shared. It was too deep. Joy had only known Debbie a short time, but those sessions of painting her as Jarius's daughter had been precious. She had become very fond of the little girl. Thank God, she would never be forgotten—she would live in the mural forever. Joy was grateful that it had been her brush and God-given talent that made that possible.

That afternoon as Joy left the hospital, a few large, wet flakes began to fall out of a gray sky lumpy with clouds. Joy felt as melancholy as the weather. She knew Gayle must be grieving dreadfully, and her heart ached for her friend. She had not tried to go back to pediatrics, look for her to try to comfort her. Death was Gayle's enemy. She would have to fight it in her own way. In spite of her fierce resistance to it, the young doctor would have to come to terms with it.

Feeling sad for her friend, wishing she could do something to ease her pain, Joy stopped at a florist's and ordered a mixed bouquet of daffodils and baby blue irises to be delivered to Gayle's apartment. She enclosed a little note:

Hyacinths for the soul. Thinking of you with affectionate concern.

Always your friend,
Joy Montrose

chapter

22

"I'VE GOT YOUR model for you," Ginny told Joy, coming into the solarium one morning.

Joy, who had been staring at the unfinished panel, whirled around. "Who?"

"His name is Todd Nelson. He's a musician. A classical guitarist. His eye was injured in an automobile accident—he went through the windshield, I think, and the glass splintered. It was pretty bad, I guess. He's just undergone surgery, and it's uncertain whether he'll recover the sight in his eye."

"Is he willing to pose?" was Joy's question.

"I've told him about the mural and about you. He's anxious to meet *you*"—Ginny winked—"and see the mural, of course. So? Wasn't I brilliant to find him for you?"

Joy gave Ginny a knowing look. "As long as you aren't trying to play matchmaker."

"Who, me?" Ginny laughed. "Shall I bring him in?"

"Sure, why not?" Joy said, smiling.

Todd turned out to be a wonderful model and an interesting person. He was young and tall, and his injured eye was covered with a white bandage. He seemed to be making a conscious effort to be optimistic, but Joy could sense that he was troubled about his prognosis. However, he was enthusiastic about his music career and empathetic to Joy's feelings about her art. He had been to Europe before the car accident and gave Joy several good travel tips about inexpensive places to stay and places to go.

"We rented bikes and had a wonderful trip through Provence," he told her. "I know you'd enjoy something like that."

"First I'm going to London, to the Tate and National Galleries, then of course to Paris," Joy told him. "To the Louvre, naturally. After that I plan to join a painting group going on a tour to the south of France. Then maybe I'll branch off by myself."

The modeling sessions with Todd became something Joy looked forward to every day, and she was almost sorry when the panel was completed.

It would be several more weeks before Todd would know if the operation on his eye would be successful, but he promised to keep in touch with Joy and let her know.

The day he left the hospital, he came to say good-bye. She gave him an impulsive hug, saying, "I'll be praying for another miracle."

He grinned. "Thanks, Joy. I think maybe the miracle's already happened. Posing for the panel has restored my spirit. I've been composing a new song."

Joy felt happy about the panel, considering it to be perhaps the best of the five. Except for the centurion. In her heart Joy thought that was the best painting she had ever done.

She did not know what Evan really thought of it. Since her return from Mayfield he had kept his distance. He never came by the solarium anymore. As he promised, he was meeting her terms. He took nothing for granted. He always called ahead to invite her, in the most casual way, out to dinner or to a movie or a concert. When they were together, he never brought up the subject of marriage. On the surface at least, he seemed to have accepted the fact that Joy was going on with her own plans.

For all his well-maintained cool, Joy knew she had hurt him. She made an appointment to talk to Sister Mary Hope again.

"I never meant to hurt him. I never meant to have him fall in love with me. It simply happened. I just had to choose. And what I've chosen has hurt him badly."

"Sometimes we can't avoid hurting someone else, even when we don't want to. Or being hurt ourselves," Sister Mary Hope said gently. "You did what you felt was the honest, right thing. That's all anyone can be expected to do. Surely Dr. Wallace knows that life deals all of us unexpected blows. It's a measure of his maturity that he has accepted your decision."

Joy longed to confide in Gayle. But Gayle was remote, locked in her own battle to accept her loss. She turned down Joy's suggestions for having lunch or supper together. Joy ached for her friend but finally thought it best to leave her to work things out herself.

She did, however, talk to Ginny Stratton, who had dealt with her own struggle to get over her dead-end affair. "Everyone gets hurt at some time or other. There are no guarantees that life is going to hand out happiness like Popsicles. I guess it all evens out somehow."

"That's almost exactly what Sister Mary Hope said!" Joy looked at her in astonishment.

"So I'm getting some wisdom in my old age," quipped Ginny, rolling her eyes.

Maybe it would just take time, Joy decided. Once she was gone, Evan would get over his hurt.

The mural was to be dedicated in the first week of May. When the date was set, Joy was still putting the finishing touches on each one, applying the final glaze. Understandably, she was apprehensive. Even though she believed the panels were her best work, even though she knew she had poured herself into them. Still, to have them open to public, possibly critical opinion was daunting. Every brushstroke had been a statement of faith. Yet as every artist knows, the finished work does not always measure up to the original vision. There were some things Joy might have changed, especially about the early panels, if she had the opportunity. But the panel of Jarius's daughter had become a memorial to little Debbie, and Joy could not help but secretly be especially proud of the centurion.

As the date drew nearer, Joy occupied herself with travel plans. She had an agent map out an itinerary which would allow her time on her own before meeting the painting group with whom she was going to tour in France. She shopped for clothes that would be easy to pack—washable, not easily wrinkled—and good, practical walking shoes. The woman at the travel agency assured her that nowadays almost anything she forgot would be available and easy to buy overseas.

Sometimes Joy could hardly believe that all this was really happening, that she was actually going to fulfill her dream.

She missed Gayle terribly. Even though it had been over a month since little Debbie's death, Gayle remained sealed in her inaccessible cocoon. Joy did not feel free to intrude on her friend's grief, but she worried and prayed for her. She hoped they could renew their friendship before she left for Europe.

Invitations to the dedication ceremony had been beautifully designed and printed and were being delivered to community leaders and other dignitaries. Joy went by Dr. Fonteyne's office to pick up a batch so she could send them out to people on her own list.

"You should be so proud, Joy," said Dr. Fonteyne's secretary, Sylvia. "Everyone who sees the mural raves about it. To be truthful, I wasn't sure what it would really be like even after you showed me the sketches, but you've certainly outdone yourself and exceeded everyone's expectations."

Pleased but humbled by all the praise, Joy thanked her. "It was a wonderful time for me. I'll miss the hospital and all the staff. Everyone's been so kind."

"We'll miss you, too, Joy." Sylvia gave her a pointed look. "Some more than others, I expect."

Joy felt herself blushing. Had Sylvia heard rumors about her and Evan? Probably. Well, it couldn't be helped—and anyway, now it was over. She needn't worry about it anymore.

Joy had not been home long and had just started to address some of the invitations when the phone rang. It was Gayle.

"Want to go to church with me on Sunday?" Gayle asked.

Surprised and touched, Joy answered, "Oh yes. I'd like that."

The small church to which Gayle took Joy when Sunday came was filled with a diversified congregation—people of all ages, colors, and ethnic backgrounds. The atmosphere was warm and friendly, with everyone greeting everyone else as if they had all known each other forever.

There was a long worship segment, followed by a thoughtful sermon. The Communion service was preceded by the singing of one of the loveliest of hymns, "Let Us Break Bread Together on Our Knees."

Let us break bread together on our knees.
When I fall on my knees with my face to the rising sun,
May the Lord have mercy on me.
We will praise God together on our knees. . . .

There followed a few moments of meditation, after which the minister suggested, "Anyone who has a special need or is heart weary or burdened in any way is welcome to come to the altar and be prayed for." Joy was a little surprised to see Gayle go forward. She knew her to be such a private person that she wondered at this public acknowledgment of need.

Joy saw Gayle kneel, head bowed over clasped hands, then saw two middle-aged women, one white, one black, go to her, gently lay hands on her bent shoulders. Joy realized the young doctor was weeping. Of course, Gayle had brought her struggle with Debbie's death to be surrendered, lifted up, to have her sorrow healed in a special way. Although Gayle never spoke of it openly, Joy realized her deep spirituality, her sense of calling to be a physician, and the need she now recognized. Joy felt blessed by Gayle's faith and her friendship.

chapter

23

AT LAST THE DAY for the dedication of the mural had come. There had been a small informal unveiling for the selection committee, and the members had all been complimentary. But now it was time for the formal unveiling and reception. The public, the press, members of the hospital board, sponsors, and civic dignitaries had all been invited to attend the ceremony.

Reporters from the newspaper and local TV stations would be interviewing. Sister Mary Hope had warned Joy to be prepared for questions. The very thought of that chilled Joy. She was both excited and more than a little nervous.

Molly had come for the occasion, and she and Joy arrived together to find the solarium crowded to the edges. It was glaringly bright with the extra lights of the television crews on hand to film the event for the local six o'clock news. The doors to the solarium had been left open so that ambulatory and wheelchair patients could see the goings on as well.

Joy could hardly believe it was over. Nearly a year of her life had gone into the mural. A year of unimaginable change. Not only had she achieved professional success in painting the mural, but there had been the unexpected inheritance of Montclair, and the fulfillment of her dream to travel abroad. Her reservations were made, and she was leaving for Europe the following week. There remained only one tiny seed of sadness deep within. Evan. She deliberately tried not to dwell on her emotions about him. She did not dare.

Flashbulbs popped as some of the guests took pictures of the mural. Joy blinked dazedly as Dr. Fonteyne greeted her. "Come along, my dear, you're the real star of the show. I want to introduce you so everyone will know whom to congratulate."

Leaving Molly in the good company of Gayle and Sister Mary Hope, Joy let him lead her up to where a podium and microphone had been placed. Joy's heart was thumping wildly as Dr. Fonteyne began his speech.

"This beautiful mural will be a permanent source of inspiration to all the doctors and staff of this hospital as they treat suffering human beings who come here seeking help. It will serve as a reminder to all who strive in the healing arts that there is a Great Physician whose power surpasses all man's meager efforts.

"It will provide comfort and hope to the patients' family and friends who wait here as we with our human skills and with divine assistance try to achieve successful results.

"Last but certainly not least, we must credit the remarkable talent of the young artist who created these panels, Miss Joy Montrose."

Here he gestured to her and there followed a burst of applause. Dr. Fonteyne let it continue for a few minutes, then held up his hand for quiet. "So we dedicate this mural today and invite all here to examine it, meet and congratulate Miss Montrose, partake of refreshments, and enjoy this time with us."

The quiet of the crowd broke into a buzz of voices and laughter as people began to form a line in front of the mural. Immediately people came up to Joy. Debbie's parents were among the first. Mrs. Matthews hugged her, saying, "Somehow you've given Debbie back to us in a way. Thank you." Mr. Matthews' dark eyes glistened as he shook Joy's hand.

Moira Andrews, elegantly dressed and exquisitely coifed as usual, embraced Joy. "My time spent posing with you changed my life—it really did, my dear." There wasn't time to explore that further, but Moira pressed a small, beautifully wrapped package into Joy's hands. "A little something for your trip. God bless you."

Philip Kenan was also there, walking pretty well with only a cane. He gruffly congratulated Joy. "Well done, young lady."

A tall young man approached Joy. At first she did not recognize him without his bandage. When she realized it was Todd Nelson, she exclaimed, "Todd, your eye! You can see!"

"Yes, just like in 'Amazing Grace'—once I was blind but now I can see. In more ways than one, Joy." He shook her hand and, still holding it, said, "I want you to meet my fiancée."

The pretty girl with him told her, "I've been so anxious to meet you. You've done so much for Todd. He was terribly depressed after his surgery, but posing for the panel—well, all I can say is, it was a miracle. Even before they knew the surgery was successful, his whole attitude changed. Thank you."

Joy met Todd's clear gaze. They knew what miracle had happened.

A stream of others came also, several of whom Joy vaguely recognized. Some told her that they had been patients at Good Samaritan while she was working on the mural and that watching her had whiled away the tedious hours of recovery. Many nurses and doctors were among those congratulating her. The response was almost too much. Joy began to feel an emotional overload. She moved over to the doors that led out onto the deck, feeling the need for some fresh air.

"Joy." She heard the familiar voice speak her name, and she whirled around to see Evan. He must have seen her leave and followed her out from the crowded solarium.

His eyes swept over her. "Congratulations. You deserve everything people are saying about it."

"Thank you, but you are a part of it, too, you know."

"The centurion? That's not me. That's your idea of what I might be if I—" He halted. "So you'll be leaving next week." He paused. "May I take you to the airport?"

Joy shook her head. "No, thank you, Evan. Molly's here and she plans to take me. She's staying after I go, to close up the apartment for me."

"Oh, I see. Well . . . can I come see you off?"

Joy bit her lower lip, feeling unhappy, then said, "I don't think that's a good idea, Evan."

He hesitated. "I don't want you to go, Joy. I'm afraid that you won't come back, that I'll never see you again."

"Of course you will, Evan. Of course I'll be back," Joy protested. She was about to say more, but just then Dr. Fonteyne came out on the deck, accompanied by a well-dressed couple.

"Ah, Miss Montrose, here you are. The mayor and his wife want to meet you."

By the time introductions were made and pleasantries exchanged, Joy realized that Evan had left. She looked around but he was gone. There was nothing she could do.

Joy entered the huge terminal at New York International Airport, checked the direction board, then headed for the escalator. Her heart was hammering loudly. This was it at last. She was really on her way. She stepped off the escalator at the top and went along the moving walkway to the gates that led to the lounge for international flights. She verified her flight number, looked for the correct gate, then advanced through security. She pulled her ticket out of the handsome leather shoulder bag Evan had given her and moved to join the line of people waiting at the check-in counter.

Was this really happening? It still felt unreal. She was given a boarding pass, and her suitcase was tagged and weighed.

Then she glanced around, searching for a seat in the crowded lounge. She had just started toward an empty chair when she was startled to hear her name over the PA system.

"Miss Joy Montrose, courtesy phone. Miss Montrose, please go to the nearest white courtesy phone. Call waiting."

She halted, set down her bag, listened. The announcement came again. She hesitated, then checked her watch. Who could be calling? Molly? Joy had just spoken with her four hours ago when Molly had seen her off to New York.

Evan? She looked at her watch again. Evan might just be getting out of O.R. He had taken Joy and Molly out to dinner the night before, and they'd said good-bye.

The announcement was repeated a third time. Joy shifted her shoulder strap and hurried toward the white courtesy phone.

It was Evan. "Couldn't let you go without telling you that I'm really happy you're getting to do this, Joy. I just don't want you to forget me. I want you to come back." His voice sounded strange, faraway. Miles already separated them, and soon there would be an ocean ... Her fingers tightened on the receiver.

An announcement echoed through the building. "British Airways flight number 647 now boarding."

Joy stiffened. "Evan, I have to go. They've just announced my flight." She looked over her shoulder. The line of people was beginning to move toward the door leading down the ramp. The announcement was repeated.

"Joy, I just wanted you to know I love you." Evan's voice was husky. She knew what he was waiting for, hoping she would say. But she could not say it.

"Thank you, Evan, for calling, for everything. I have to go now. Good-bye." She hung up and hurried to the quickly diminishing line of fellow passengers, her pulse racing with excitement. She did not know what lay ahead. She only knew what she had left behind.

chapter
24

Dear Molly,

I'm on my way, airborne over the Atlantic. Looking down, all I can see are mountains of clouds, and I'm floating on number nine! Thank you from the bottom of my heart for encouraging me to have this dream, strengthening my belief that it could come true, and helping me accomplish it. I only wish you could be sharing it all with me. I will try to keep notes, remember everything I see that I think you would be interested in hearing about. Thank you for the rolls of film you stuck in my purse—I promise I'll keep my camera loaded and bring lots of pictures back to share this wonderful experience with you. They are serving luncheon now. Seems as if I just ate. However, it looks delicious, so I'll close for now. More later from London!

Always,
Joy

Dear Molly,

London is fabulous. I have saturated myself with hours spent at the Tate and National Galleries and still have not seen everything I wanted to or absorbed it all.

To be able to get close enough to see brushstrokes on these masterpieces, to just sit and stare at them, is fantastic.

The light captured in Turner's landscapes, the English countryside painted by Constable, makes you want to walk along the roads yourself. Whistler, of course, and I spent hours viewing Millais's and Rossetti's paintings. What an experience this is.

Dear Ginny,

Couldn't resist this postcard from the National Gallery. When you accuse me of being impractical and a dreamer, remember: "The most beautiful things in the world are useless: peacocks and lilies, for instance"—John Ruskin.

Dear Gayle,

I'm sure you'll be interested to know that I took the train down to Kentburne to see what I could find out about my English ancestors. Birchfields is now called the Faith Devlin Montrose Nursing School, and there is a small teaching hospital nearby. In the courtyard is a statue of Florence Nightingale, and inside, a smaller one representing "The Valiant Army Field Nurses 1916–1918." There's a list of names including Katherine Cameron Traherne. That's Cara Montrose's twin sister, remember from the scrapbook at Montclair? The sculptress was Bryanne Montrose Colby. My family seems to turn up everywhere!

Dear Molly,

I know you're always searching for something to write in calligraphy, so I'm sending you this poem, which is written on the wall of a quaint little village church in Upwaltham.

I will not wish thee riches nor the glow of greatness,
But that wherever thou go
Some weary heart shall gladden at thy smile,
Or shadowed life know sunshine for a while,

206

And so thy path shall be a track of light,
Like angels' footsteps passing through the night.

Dear Molly,

Paris truly is the city of light. Hard to explain, but it's easy to see why artists once flourished here and still do. Many set up their easels along the way to the cathedral in Montmarte and on the banks of the Seine. It is all so picturesque, I itch to do the same. But right now there is so much to see that I shall have to wait until I join the group tour next week. I am on my way to the Louvre today. Au revoir!

Dear Molly,

Corot, Courbet, Matisse, Renoir, Degas. All the names I've known ever since I first became aware of such artists and their work. How I pored over reproductions of their paintings in art books. Now to see them! The colors, the way they come to life before your eyes! It all seems so natural, so easy, when of course they sketched, labored, repainted, and began all over again. Yet the end result are these masterpieces.

Dear Molly,

I am exhausted. In fact, I've never been this tired in my entire life. Yet I'm exhilarated! I am so alive with all I am seeing, soaking in. Tomorrow I meet with the group of painters and we're off to Arles. Imagine! To walk the same streets as Van Gogh and Gauguin, see the pastures and houses they painted.

There are fifteen of us altogether in our group, men and women, all ages, all eager to get started on this exciting journey. We board the bus with our bundles of brushes, paints, colored pencils, portable easels—a ragtag-looking bunch. There is a lot of joking and laughter. I believe it will be a fun group to be with. The two leaders of this tour are well known to some but new to me. They are New York artists and exhibit there. Our bus driver is a comedian and keeps up a lively narration—in English but liberally sprinkled with French, so that we are all picking up his way of speaking to each other. It is a hilarious mix, and we are all having a good time. Anxious to get started on some painting.

Dear Molly,

Am working mostly with watercolor. It is the easiest medium and more spontaneous than colored pencils, with which I tend to get too detailed. We are urged to work quickly, get down impressions, washes of color on which we can later work in our studios for more finished paintings.

Every evening, after we have a leisurely dinner "en famille," one of the two leaders offers a critique of our day's efforts. This is very helpful. We learn from each other's work.

Dear Molly,

I haven't written much because I have been too busy painting as much as I can. What an opportunity! I want to make the most of my time under the guidance of these two incredible artists. I am enjoying getting to know the other members of the group. We have all gotten along so well, it will be hard to say good-bye when it is time for us to go our separate ways. My sketchbook and portfolio are getting full. I think I shall bundle up most of what I've done and mail it to you so that I won't be porting it around for the rest of my trip. Hope that's okay. You can open it and look through what I've done. I think you'll be pleased.

Dear Molly,

Tonight was our last night together. It was sort of sad but also a happy occasion. We exchanged addresses and promises to keep in touch, perhaps even to meet again for another painting tour next year, maybe in Italy or Spain. I shall always be grateful for this opportunity not only to meet some wonderful fellow artists but also to learn some new and useful painting techniques.

After saying good-bye to the members of the group upon returning to Paris, Joy decided to take Todd Nelson's suggestion and go to Provence, rent a bike, and take a cycling trip through the region.

She was still experiencing the stimulation of the painting tour, and it wasn't until the second day of her bike trip that Joy felt a letdown. It wasn't the scenery or the weather that caused it. They were both beautiful. Late summer in the south of France was spectacular. It was being alone. She missed the interaction and camaraderie of being with her painting companions. But more than that, she wanted someone with whom to share her experience.

As she pedaled, she recalled Evan's offer: "I'll take you to Europe, to France, Italy, anywhere you want to go." He would be a wonderful traveling companion. She imagined them roaming the French countryside together, taking serendipitous side trips.

She knew that Evan would have researched the area and its history beforehand, that he loved exploring, and eating different foods in out-of-the-way little restaurants. She knew he would appreciate the novelty of it all.

Traveling in Europe with him would be special, interesting, enjoyable. The more she tried to put it out of her mind, the more insistent the thought became. It was Evan she missed.

Fiercely she pedaled, trying not to think of him. *This is what I wanted, isn't it? Being free? Living like a gypsy with no responsibilities. In France on my own.* Hadn't she dreamed of staying in little country pensions, eating bread and cheese and fruit, stopping anywhere to paint? That's what she wanted. Or what she thought she wanted.

But did she really want to be alone?

chapter
25

THE SOLARIUM WAS dimly lit by the light from the corridor and by lights shining up from the parking lot outside. Still in his green scrub suit, Evan sat down on one of the leather sofas facing the mural. His shoulders slumped wearily, and he placed his head in his hands. He wasn't sure how long he remained there, physically exhausted, mentally drained. Slowly he lifted his head and gazed up at one of the panels. The blind man receiving his sight. A mix of emotions warred within Evan— anger, resentment, frustration. Anger that all his skill had not been able to save his patient, resentment that nothing they had attempted had stopped the inevitable, frustration that there was nothing more anyone could have done to bring life back into the body on the operating table.

Why? Why had he failed? The operation had not been that complicated. He had performed it dozens of times. Why had all the latest scientific tools not been enough? All the same helplessness he had felt when Susan died came rushing back. He experienced it all again in vivid detail. It was all such a waste. The man he had operated on had a reasonably long life ahead of him. Was there no purpose to any of it?

His gaze moved from panel to panel. It halted at the centurion's scene. The final rendering had been different from the

one for which he had originally posed. Now the Roman officer knelt on one knee, bowing his head to Jesus, the Jewish
healer. Why had Joy changed it?

Evan remembered asking her about it, and at the time her
reply had not been understandable to him: "It just seemed more
appropriate. It was prophesied that every knee shall bow at the
name of Jesus. The centurion had come to beg mercy for his servant, not stand arrogantly as though he deserved the favor."

Evan hadn't pursued the subject. Instinctively he had felt
that Joy was trying to tell him something about himself.
Something about his own attitude, maybe?

He returned to the scene of the blind man. "Once I was
blind but now I see"—those were the words painted at the
bottom of the panel. He remembered those words from his
days long ago in Sunday school in the little Kentucky church
in the mining town where he had grown up. He recalled
singing the words very loudly, trying to outdo his buddy Jason
during the hymn "Amazing Grace." He thought about the
phrase "God's amazing grace" and recalled another of those
disturbing conversations he'd had with Joy. He had come in
here one evening when she was just finishing up and looking
over her day's work on the healing of the paralytic, the panel
for which his patient Philip Kenan had posed, and he had
asked, "Why did Jesus often say, 'Your sins are forgiven' when
he was only asked for healing?"

"Sometimes it's hidden sin, such as unforgiveness, that
blocks God's blessing," Joy had answered. Then she had
turned to him with a puzzled frown. "I should think that as a
doctor, you'd know there is more and more proof that negative emotions hinder healing. Hatred, anger, bitterness, that
sort of thing."

Again Evan had dropped the subject. Sometimes Joy, for all
her sweetness, her gentleness, hit too close to the mark. She

knew he was still wounded by his inability to save Susan. Her death had unfairly cut off a vital, useful life. And it was that unfairness that he hated. The hatred was a grinding pain within, like a cancer that needed to be cut out. But against what or who was the hatred directed?

Tonight he couldn't seem to take his gaze away from the paintings. Each one had a special significance, and each person looking at them might see something different. He realized the mural must be a comfort, a blessing, for the family and friends of patients as they waited here. Being reminded of these healing miracles must renew their hope, strengthen their faith. The panels did not seem to offer false hope, as he had once remarked.

God, whoever you are, wherever you are, let these paintings be the blessing Joy has painted them to be.

He thought of Joy and his heart ached. He missed her so much, in every way. He knew he loved her, but he had fallen short of what she wanted in a life partner. He had offered her everything he possessed—the security, the affluence, that came with being at the top of his profession. He had promised her freedom to pursue her art even if it meant travel, time away from him. Whatever he had, whatever it would take to possess this treasure of a woman. He thought he could overcome those doubts, those uncertainties she had—what she called being "unequally yoked." Whatever that meant! It could have worked. Her faith was strong enough for both of them. He wouldn't stand in her way if she wanted to go to church three times a week, twice a day, whatever! But that hadn't been enough to convince her.

As he continued to sit there in the dimness of the empty solarium, Evan knew it was not enough. One by one he returned to each panel. The little girl, the paralytic, Peter's mother-in-law, the centurion, the blind man . . . What was keeping him from seeing what Joy saw?

213

Suddenly it came to him so clearly, like the scales being removed from a blind man's eyes. It was his own bitterness against God because of Susan's death. Yes, that was it! That was why he couldn't believe. It was the reason why he felt shut out from the peace, the hope, the faith—from Joy. All the old anger merged with anguish.

But I want to be free of it. I want to be forgiven . . .

Evan realized he had just prayed. He raked his fingers through his hair, shuddering. He looked at the centurion panel—and he saw his own pride, his arrogance, his unwillingness to surrender, everything that made faith so difficult for him.

He clenched his hands together tightly. He felt a twisting sensation, a longing to let go, to surrender himself and all the angry sadness inside.

Then out of somewhere—he must have read it or heard it at some time—the direction came so that there could be no mistake.

"Physician, heal thyself."

Evan started, looked around. Who had spoken? His tiredness was playing mind games on him, he thought. But the words came once more from an almost forgotten source.

"Physician, heal thyself."

Nothing would happen until then. There could be no reconciliation, no forgiveness, no faith, no future with Joy . . . until, as in that painting in her apartment, he opened that door without a handle, the door that invited God into the human heart.

The longer Evan sat there, the more significant the thought became. Gradually he felt as if a tight band around his chest had loosened and he could draw a deep breath.

He gazed at the painting of the centurion, and he finally understood why Joy had changed the man's position. That is how you ask for healing, for forgiveness. On your knees.

Evan gave a self-conscious look over both shoulders. Then he slipped down and knelt.

chapter
26

AT THE END of September Joy flew home. Throughout the flight her emotions were a jumble. Excitement mixed with apprehension. Molly had written to say that Evan had kept in touch with her—that he had in fact "badgered her," as Molly so humorously put it. He had insisted on meeting her flight, and Joy wondered how she would feel when she saw him.

Her feelings had gone through several changes while she was abroad. When she picked up her mail at the American consulate's office in Paris, there was always a letter from Evan. His handwriting was a typically illegible doctor's scrawl. Yet the few scribbled lines in each note somehow lodged in Joy's heart, confirming his love for her.

> *I miss you terribly, long to see you, but I am also glad you are having this chance.*

In return she had sent him postcards, usually ones she bought at the gallery and museum gift shops. At Saint Paul's Cathedral she had purchased a postcard with a reproduction of Holman Hunt's *Light of the World*.

> *Dear Evan,*
> *I have fulfilled one of my dreams. I've now seen the orig-inal. It is magnificent.*

There would be much to tell him when she saw him. She had never realized how much there would be to talk about when she returned. So much had happened within her these past months. What had happened with Evan?

She decided she would try to sleep, not think. She bunched the small pillow underneath her head and closed her eyes. She realized she had drifted off when she was awakened by the flight attendant bringing her a small, dampened towel to refresh her face and saying, "We'll be landing in about twenty minutes."

Joy adjusted her seat to an upright position and looked out the window. Clouds were breaking up below, and here and there she saw roads, rooftops, highways with cars and trucks moving along like toys. She felt tingly all over. How would it be when she saw Evan again?

She heard the thump of tires on the tarmac, felt the rush of deceleration. As the plane slowly maneuvered to its place next to the terminal, outside her window Joy saw airline personnel run across the landing field, a baggage truck swing into place at the side of the plane. She gathered her belongings, including her tote bag full of brochures and souvenirs, got up from her seat, moved out into the crowded aisle, and slowly made her way to the door. She thanked the flight attendant, then walked up the enclosed ramp into the terminal. All the time her heart was pounding.

Then at last into the waiting lounge and into Evan's arms. They hugged and laughed. He held her at arm's length, looking at her. "It's so good to see you!" he said over and over.

There would be at least a half hour's wait for luggage. So they went into one of the airport restaurants. They found a table, ordered sandwiches and sodas, Joy wasn't sure what kind. The frenetic activity, the buzz of conversation, swirled around them. They just sat, smiling at each other. When their order came, Joy didn't even notice what she was eating.

Sitting opposite him, she was very much aware that there was something different about Evan. It was subtle but significant. Something had taken place during the last four months. Something, Joy felt sure, he would soon tell her about. He seemed bursting with a new kind of enthusiasm. When nothing was forthcoming, she grew curious. But there wasn't time, and neither was this noisy airport restaurant the place. They picked up Joy's luggage and went to the level of the airport garage where Evan had parked his car.

On the way to Joy's apartment, Evan said, "I talked to Molly yesterday, and she said to tell you that she came up and aired out your apartment, brought in some staples, put stuff in the refrigerator." He paused. "She also said the contractor in Mayfield was in touch with her, and the cottage roof has been repaired and all the interior painting is done." Evan glanced over at her. "I hope that doesn't mean you're moving to Virginia?"

Joy laughed. "You know better than that. The big house and most of the grounds are going to the Mayfield Historical Society. She means another small building on the property."

"I see," Evan said, nodding. He looked serious. "Molly says it's an idyllic spot for an artist."

"Yes, for a vacation or a retreat. Actually, it's too isolated for year-round living. Besides, I have to find a job."

"Oh? I thought you'd become a lady of leisure now that you're an heiress."

"Of course not, Evan. I've learned so much about art this summer. I'm all charged up about the possibilities of what I can do to make my living. After being in the galleries in London and Paris, I've also learned my artistic limitations."

"The mural is still getting rave reviews."

"Is it? I'm so glad. I'll probably see things I'd like to do over now that I've been exposed to master works."

217

"Speaking of jobs, there's something I want to talk to you about. I have a project in mind."

They had reached the tree house, and Evan carried Joy's baggage up the stairway. She walked inside and slowly circled the small room, saying, "Everything looks so . . . so unfamiliar!"

"It'll take time to reacclimate yourself." Evan watched her as she moved about the tiny place, touching things as if to reacquaint herself with her former environment.

"Now, tell me about your project," Joy suggested. "I will have to get started on something soon." She pulled a comic face. "I was terribly extravagant on my trip. Sit down, let's talk about it." She gestured to the two wicker chairs in the window area.

"Well," Evan began as he sat, "I've always wanted to do something in Susan's memory. Something permanent, something that would really represent her, the kind of person she was, the way she lived her life. She was the most generous person I've ever known—helping people was her calling. So I've come up with what I think it should be. Now that I can afford it, I'd like to build a hospice, like the kind they have in England. A place where terminal patients can go, where they'll be treated with kindness, dignity, true loving care. The kind of care Susan always gave her patients."

Joy was astonished. This was the first time Evan had mentioned Susan without a trace of bitterness. Instead he seemed happy and enthusiastic about his idea.

"I'm going to get Glendon McFarland—you know, the architect who designed the solarium at the hospital—to draw up the plans. I told him my ideas, gave him some rough sketches of what I have in mind. Everything will be light, airy, lots of windows. An atrium, maybe a fountain, in the center of the reception hall, beautiful landscaped gardens that can be seen from every room. And the rooms will have beautiful paintings, murals with peaceful, hopeful scenes." He halted, eyes twinkling. "That is, if I can find the right artist for the job."

"Are you making me an offer I can't refuse?" Joy asked.

"Maybe. Are you interested?"

"I've often thought I'd like to paint the parables of Jesus in a mural. Would something like that be acceptable? Or would I have to make a presentation to a selection committee?"

"A committee of one," Evan replied, grinning. Impulsively he sat forward and reached for her hands. "Oh, Joy, it's so good to have you back. I can't tell you what my life has been with you gone. Colorless, gray, drab. I'd go to the hospital, come home, stare at the TV without knowing what I was watching, think about you, where you were, what you were doing, if you'd met anyone." He pressed her hands. "Did you?"

"You mean some stranger across a crowded room? No." She shook her head, smiling.

He continued. "Sometimes I'd go back to the hospital at night to check on some of my patients, and then I'd go into the solarium and look at the mural. I'd look at each panel, try to figure out what had really taken place in those scenes. Especially the painting of the centurion. I'd ask myself why you changed it, painted it differently from the sketch you had originally decided on. I'd ask myself if there was some hidden message there for me."

"And . . . was there?"

Evan's hold on her hands tightened. "'Physician, heal thyself.'" He paused. "A few days later I got the postcard you sent with the picture of *The Light of the World,* and I guess you might say I got it. I finally got it. I went back and studied the mural. And something happened. Inside me. I can't describe it exactly, except to say that I felt a kind of loosening of a lot of old stuff, an opening to what life might be if I let go. It was as if a tight band around my chest snapped."

Evan's voice deepened, and he struggled for words to go on. "I realized that there was a lot of leftover junk from the past. Stuff that was making it impossible for me to understand God's love. Why had he taken Susan? Then I began to understand that it wasn't up to me to figure that out. Maybe it was to save her from something worse than death. I don't know. What was making me resist was that I considered it too easy. Cheap grace, I think they call it. Just accept, let it go. Allow God's love to heal me."

Joy was too moved to say anything.

"Something else I found out, Joy, was that I'd made a mistake about us."

Startled, Joy wasn't sure what was coming next.

"I thought that I could convince you to marry me, that I could lean on your faith, that it would be enough. But now I know I had to find the key myself to open the door of my heart to God." Evan turned and pointed to the picture of *The Light of the World*. "The key to open that door was getting rid of resentment, bitterness, asking forgiveness for what I'd been holding against him. Once I did that, the love just kind of exploded in me." He brought one of her hands to his lips, kissed the fingertips. "I felt free, Joy, to love you completely. So much more than I ever thought possible."

Joy's heart was too full to speak. She leaned forward and kissed Evan, a kiss that was loving and full of tender promise.

chapter

27

PLANS FOR THE Susan Wallace Memorial went forward, and Joy was in on most of the meetings with the architect and builder. Her suggestions and ideas were respectfully heard and accepted.

With a new confidence and a heart full of hope and gladness for the change that had come to Evan, Joy started work on her part of the hospice. She didn't want to reproduce the Good Samaritan panels; she wanted to create something new and different and representative of all the hospice would be.

She went carefully through her portfolio of sketches and quick watercolors she had done on her painting tour through the south of France. One she had done on a day when she had climbed up a rocky hill, a little too steep for most of her fellow artists, and at the crest had found a little wayside chapel of ancient stone. It had a curved door overhung with vines. Enlarged, this might be a scene she could paint in the entrance foyer. They could get Molly to do the calligraphy, using the scriptural invitation from Matthew 11:28: "Come to me, all you who are weary and burdened, and I will give you rest." Or perhaps even more appropriate for a hospice would be John 14:27: "Do not let your hearts be troubled and do not be afraid."

Evan wanted a room for prayer and meditation to be included in the architectural plans. Joy thought of another design to go on its doors, along with a quotation she had copied from the wall of a church in an English village: "We are always open for prayer. Come in and abide awhile with your Lord."

Evan was enthusiastic about all Joy's ideas and sketches and gave her a carte blanche go-ahead.

A few weeks after she returned from Europe, Joy received word from the Mayfield Historical Society that the grand opening of Montclair was scheduled for late October, and she was asked to be there. The invitation included complimentary lodging for her and a guest at the Mayfield Inn. Joy's first thought was Molly, but when she called her, Molly begged off. She had two weddings for which she had to provide hand-lettered announcements, as well as some holiday parties for which she was committed to design invitations.

"I'm swamped. Why not ask Gayle? After all, she has connections to Montclair, too."

But Gayle was unsure. Her schedule too was heavy.

"It would be lovely if you and your mother both could come," Joy suggested. "Even for one day. It would be really wonderful."

"I'll talk to her about it and see if I can get someone to cover for me. I'll let you know," Gayle promised.

Joy was experiencing such a resurgence of creative energy at that time regarding the hospice project that she felt almost reluctant to take a break and go to Mayfield.

When she told Evan about the trip, she saw an eagerness leap into his eyes. For the first time, the thought came that she would like Evan to see Montclair.

"Of course. I'll rearrange my schedule. No problem. I'd like to go," was his enthusiastic reply when she asked him to join her.

Since her return from Europe, their relationship had been delicate. Now Joy was thrilled by Evan's seeming change of attitude. There had always been a definitive air of authority about him, but now he had a quiet assurance, a new confidence that had nothing to do with his reputation or career. It came from within, and its presence filled her with awe. How God could change a person's heart was an amazing mystery.

However, she still had unresolved questions about herself, her willingness to make the commitment Evan wanted. Marriage was a big step, and Joy was not sure she was ready to take it.

Evan seemed to have no doubts. Although he hadn't brought up the subject again since her return, Joy had kept a letter he had written to her while she was away. It was only a single sheet, typed because of his bad handwriting.

You accuse me of being a skeptic. Well, I'm not about marriage. I think it is the most important thing any two people can do. I don't take it lightly. Not at all. I don't really know what you mean by being "unequally yoked." Sure, we have differences, but none that we can't work out. I have no intention of trying to change you or your beliefs.

I'm sending you this quote written by another so-called skeptic—Mark Twain—on a subject we both feel strongly about. I think this may prove we're not all that far apart.

A marriage ... makes of two fractional lives, a whole. It gives to two purposeless lives a work, and doubles the strength of each to perform it. It gives two questioning natures a reason for living, and something to live for:

It will give a new gladness to the sunshine,
A new fragrance to the flowers,
A new beauty to the earth,
And a new mystery to life.

The night before they were to leave for Mayfield, Joy reread the letter. It touched her in a deeper way than ever before. For some reason she felt that maybe seeing Montclair together would clarify things between her and Evan.

223

chapter
28

VIRGINIA IN THE FALL is spectacular. The area is famous for its autumn display, and that October the gold and crimson colors outdid themselves. The opening of Montclair to the public was held on one of the most beautiful days that year.

The renovation was complete. Furnishings and artifacts from subsequent generations had been replaced. All the brides' portraits were hung on the wall alongside the winding staircase, in chronological order. The empty rooms had been filled with appropriate, glowingly polished furniture, newly upholstered in material that matched the original coverings as closely as possible. Everything had been restored to its condition at the time when Montclair was the pride of its owners and known for its hospitality. The house was perfect. It looked as it might have when Noramary Marsh, the first bride, stepped across the threshold.

Afternoon shadows on the velvety lawn began to lengthen. The speeches had all been made, and the dignitaries had departed. Only a few visitors still lingered, as if loath to leave the beautiful setting. Some still wandered in the gardens. Joy had shaken hands with and accepted the greetings of so many people that her fingers tingled and her mouth felt stretched with smiling. She had been touched as well as amazed and thrilled that so many people in Mayfield remembered the Montrose family she herself had never known, that her ancestors and relatives had meant a great deal to the community, had made an impact and left a lasting impression. They had been proud, honorable, interesting people who had served their state and country well in various capacities. They had been people of character—settlers, farmers, soldiers, statesmen. Among them had been women of valor and gallantry who had lived their lives wisely and nobly, had loved their families, their children, and Montclair, their home.

Joy was tired but enormously pleased that everything had worked out so perfectly. The ceremony had been just long enough, the tributes and speeches just eloquent enough, and everyone attending had a feeling of satisfaction that they had seen what they had come to see—Montclair returned to its former glory, open now for all time for people to share its story, its beauty, its historic value.

A short while later, after saying good-bye to the two remaining attendees, Joy looked around and saw Evan standing at a discreet distance. He had waited patiently while she chatted with one of the guests, an elderly woman and her daughter who had known her grandmother Nicole. When they departed, he came toward her. Today he looked particularly handsome. He smiled as his gaze swept over her, and he said, "All you need is a crinoline and a parasol, and you would fit into this scene perfectly. We ought to have your portrait painted to hang on the wall with the other Montrose ladies."

"It's been an incredible day. Wasn't Gayle's mother magnificent?" she asked. Gayle had managed to make it after all and had brought her mother, a tall, lovely woman with silvery hair and bright, intelligent eyes, who spoke with dignity about her own ancestors who had lived at Montclair.

"Where are they? I thought we could all go to dinner somewhere." Evan looked around.

"They left already. Gayle had to get back, and they were going to stay overnight with some relatives on the way back. So it's just you and me."

"That's okay with me. Are you exhausted?"

"Not really . . . well, yes, in one way. But in another way I feel excited. I've found so much here. Things I never expected to find, things I didn't realize I'd missed in my life, a family heritage. Truthfully, it's been a real homecoming for me, to a home I didn't even know I had."

"Has the entire property been given to the historical society, then?"

"Not all. The twenty acres immediately surrounding the house will belong to the historical society in perpetuity." She wrinkled her nose. "I'm not exactly sure what that means. It's legalese meaning forever, I think. That's so the grounds from the gate to the house will always be available as a historic landmark. It can't be sold or changed in any way. Some of the original farmland will be leased for agriculture, and the small parcel that adjoins the Cameron property is held in my name until or if any other Montrose descendant can be located. If another heir were found, then we would decide together whether it was to be sold or whatever. The historical society would have first refusal if we decided to sell." Joy paused, then said, "There's something I'd like to show you before we leave. Actually, it's the architect's model for the main house. Would you like to see it?"

"Let's go." He held out his hand, and they started walking down the drive together.

The last rays of the sun slanted through the tall trees as they took the woodland path. They crossed the rustic wooden bridge, then followed the path that led to where the cottage was nestled in the secluded glen a few yards away.

"It was built before Montclair," Joy told Evan. They walked slowly around it. Fall wildflowers bloomed in colorful profusion.

The flagstone path up to the little porch was overgrown, and the paint was peeling on the Dutch door with its latticed window. The tarnished brass knocker was engraved with two words.

"Eden Cottage," Evan read out loud, then turned to Joy with a puzzled expression.

"The estate lawyer told me of the tradition that Montrose brides spent their first year of marriage here," she explained. "Molly had the interior painted when she was down here last summer. There wasn't enough time to do the outside. Still, its perfectly charming, isn't it? I wonder how long this has stood empty? I wonder who was the last bride to come here on her honeymoon?"

"It might have been your mother," Evan suggested.

"No, she was never here at Montclair. My father and she were married in California, in San Diego, where he took his helicopter training." It made Joy sad to think of her young parents, who had never even had a real honeymoon.

They circled the house once more. They saw the small arbor overhung with a tangle of grapevines, romantic and mysterious. Within was a seat. Evan reached for Joy's hand, and they walked in and sat down side by side. Sun filtered in through the latticework. A lovely, peace-filled quiet enveloped them.

"Joy?" Evan began slowly. "I haven't said anything, haven't pressured you. I've waited, knowing you had all this to do since you came back from France. But I haven't changed, you know. I love you, more than ever." He paused. "How about marrying me and spending *our* honeymoon here at Eden Cottage?"

Joy looked at Evan, seeing such love and tenderness in his eyes that she felt breathless. Suddenly she realized what a big part of her life he had become. His new gentleness, his patience, had been reassuring her that his inner change was real. Since she had inherited Montclair, Evan had been there for her, supportive and strong. He had offered his help, advising her on dealings with lawyers and members of the historical society, recommending his own lawyer to help her with the contracts and papers she had to sign.

It was strange that now her life, which before had been so uncertain, held a new security. Although the sale of Montclair to the historical society gave her what amounted to a small income for life, enabling her the freedom to travel and paint as she had always dreamed, suddenly that independence did not hold the same attraction. Something was missing. The same thing she had found missing when she was biking through the south of France by herself. *Someone* was missing from that picture of the future. That person, her heart told her, was Evan.

"Well?"

Evan's prompting brought Joy back from her reverie. Immediately she was sorry. She had already kept him waiting so long for her answer.

"I've been thinking about us a great deal, Evan."

"And?" There was a hint of anxiety in his voice.

"Yes, Evan, I will."

"Will *what?*" he persisted.

She turned and looked at him, saw the anxiety in his eyes change to hope. Abandoning all former doubts, she knew deep in her heart that Evan was a man she could trust with her dreams, her future, her life. She smiled and said softly, "Marry you."

Marriage for Joy had been something a long way off, somewhere in a distant, unimaginable future. Now that it was happening, it seemed so right that she and Evan would be spending the rest of their lives together.

They decided to be married in Mayfield at the community church where so many other Montrose brides through the years had taken their wedding vows. Montclair was now open for receptions, and Joy and Evan's was the first to be held there.

She and Evan were going to keep Eden Cottage and its surrounding land as their own. They would spend the next two weeks there and come back as often as possible for a time of peace and privacy in what would continue to be a busy life. The exterior had been freshly painted, and Molly and Joy spent a week there getting the inside of the cottage ready. It was in all ways the perfect place to begin a marriage.

In a place of honor was Molly's wedding gift to them. On parchment, framed in mellow wood, she had penned a wish in calligraphy—a wish that embodied all their hopes, dreams, and prayers for their life together.

> The way is long;
> Let us go together.
> The way is difficult;
> Let us help each other.
> The way is joyful;
> Let us share it.
> The way is ours alone;
> Let us go in love.
> The way opens before us . . .
> Let us begin.

Montrose Family Tree

Duncan Montrose marries Noramary Marsh
   (Son) Camerson Montrose m.   (1) Lorabeth Whitaker
                                 (2) Arden Sherwood

Graham Montrose m. Avril Dumont
   (They adopt his nephew)

Clayborn Montrose m. Sara Leighton (Three sons)
   Malcolm m.   (1) Rose Meredith
                              (Son) Jonathan
                          (2) Blythe Dorman
                              (Son) Jeffrey
   Bryson Montrose m. Garnet Cameron
   Lee Montrose m.   Dove Maitland

Jonathan Montrose m.   (1) Davida Kendall
                           (Son) Kip (Daughter) Meredith
                       (2) Phoebe McPherson
                           (Son) Fraser (Daughter) Fiona

Kip Montrose m.   (1) Eteienette Boulanger
                           (Son) Lucien
                       (2) Cara Cameron
                           (Adopted) Nicole ("Nicki")

Fraser Montrose m. Nicole

Cameron Family Tree

James and Jaqueline Cameron
  (Son) James marries Mayrian
      (Son) Logan
  (Son) Marshall m. Rebecca Buchanan
      (Son) Douglas m. Katharine Maitland
        (Twins) Rod and Stewart
        (Daughter) Garnet m. Bryson Montrose

Rod m. Blythe Montrose (Malcolm's widow)
  (Son) Scott m. Jillian Marsh
      (Son) Stewart (Daughter) Nora ("Scotty")
  (Twins) Cara and Kitty

Garnet Montrose (Bryson's widow) m. Jeremy Devlin
  (Daughter) Faith m. Jeff Montrose
      (Daughter) Lynette m. state senator Frank Maynard
      (Daughter) Cara-Lyn
      (Daughter) Bryanne m. Steven Colby
      (Son) Gareth m. Brooke Leslie
        (Daughter) Hope

Look for these titles in Jane Peart's Brides of Montclair Series
at a Christian bookstore near you!

Valiant Bride
ISBN: 0-310-66951-0

A historical romance about a young woman's choice of duty over love.

Ransomed Bride
ISBN: 0-310-66961-8

In this sequel to *Valiant Bride,* Lorabeth Whitaker flees England
and an undesirable marriage engagement.

Fortune's Bride
ISBN: 0-310-66971-5

Graham Montrose is widowed after only three months of marriage. He becomes the guardian of a 13-year-old girl, Avril. At her
coming out party, he realizes his love for his ward.

Folly's Bride
ISBN: 0-310-66981-2

In a time of social unrest, slave rebellions, and growing political
dissent, Sara, once impetuous and flirtatious, learns to overcome her
pride as she comes under the influence of Clayborn Montrose, scion
of the Montrose family and Master of Montclair.

Yankee Bride & Rebel Bride
ISBN: 0-310-66991-X

Against the turbulent backdrop of the Civil War, two beautiful
women of strength and spirit struggle for the survival of their ideals,
dreams, principles, and love. Their antagonism enacts the spiritual
crisis of their time.

Destiny's Bride

ISBN: 0-310-67021-7

Destiny's Bride is the story of Druscilla Montrose.

Jubilee Bride

ISBN: 0-310-67121-3

In honor of Queen Victoria's Diamond Jubilee, the fiftieth year of her reign, Garnet invites both sides of her aristocratic Virginia family to England for a family reunion celebration.

Mirror Bride

ISBN: 0-310-67131-0

Mishap, romance, and mistaken identity are the ingredients for enlivening Virginia's prestigious Montrose family.

Hero's Bride

ISBN: 0-310-67141-8

The First World War is a time of testing and commitment as the eldest son goes to France to fight.

Daring Bride

ISBN: 0-310-20209-4

With the Depression clouding the present and World War II looming on the horizon, Aunt Garnet's ninetieth birthday is a reunion time for the Montrose and Cameron families.

Courageous Bride

ISBN: 0-310-20210-8

The First World War left Niki an orphan in France. Will World War II take away everything she holds dear — including Montclair, the only home she's ever known, and Fraser, the man she's grown to love?

ZondervanPublishingHouse

Grand Rapids, Michigan

A Division of HarperCollinsPublishers

Runaway Heart

ISBN: 0-310-41271-4

Heroine Holly Lambeth has escaped the humiliation of a broken engagement by visiting her cousin's family in Riverbend, Oregon. When her cousin proves less than hospitable, Holly is forced to find her own way in this very alien hostile culture.

Promise of the Valley

ISBN: 0-310-41281-1

When Southern-born Adelaide Pride follows her Yankee employer to California, she faces a private civil war and reexamines her values of love and honor.

Where Tomorrow Waits

ISBN: 0-310-41291-9

When calamity strikes, young Penny Sayres doubts her decision to trade the security of love for the adventure on the Oregon Trail.

A Distant Dawn

ISBN: 0-310-41301-X

When headstrong Sunny sets off to join the wagon train to California, she finds more adventure than she had planned.

Undaunted Spirit

ISBN: 0-310-22012-2

When Mindy McClaren finds her ambition to be a newspaper reporter squashed in her hometown, she heads for Coarse Gold, Colorado—where her passion for "the whole story" is put to the test.

The Pattern
ISBN: 0-310-20166-7

Prior to the Civil War, well-to-do Johanna marries a doctor from a poor family and moves to the harsh mountains of North Carolina.

The Pledge
ISBN: 0-310-20167-5

Johanna's daughter falls in love with a seminary student who is cast out from the southern community when he chooses to fight for the North.

The Promise
ISBN: 0-310-20168-3

Josie's daughter grows up in California and falls in love with a missionary who marries her and takes her to Hawaii, where adventures await them.

ZondervanPublishingHouse
Grand Rapids, Michigan

A Division of HarperCollins*Publishers*

We want to hear from you. Please send your comments about this book to us in care of the address below. Thank you.

ZondervanPublishingHouse
Grand Rapids, Michigan 49530
http://www.zondervan.com